Nightmare in Nagano

Roy MacGregor

M&S

An M&S Paperback Original from
McClelland & Stewart Inc.
The Canadian Publishers

PS8575. G84 N56 1998

CURRIC

For the readers who write back

The author is grateful to Doug Gibson, who thought up this
series, and to Alex Schultz, who pulls it off.

An M&S Paperback Original from
McClelland & Stewart Inc.

Canadian Cataloguing in Publication Data

MacGregor, Roy, 1948–
    Nightmare in Nagano

(The Screech Owls series)
"An M&S paperback original."
ISBN 0-7710-5619-2

I. Title.   II. Series: MacGregor, Roy, 1948– .
The Screech Owls series.

PS8575.G84N53 1998   jC813'.54   C98-932056-1
PZ7.M32Ni 1998

We acknowledge the financial support of the Government of
Canada through the Book Publishing Industry Development
Program for our publishing activities. We further acknowledge
the support of the Canada Council for the Arts and the Ontario
Arts Council for our publishing program.

Cover illustration by Gregory C. Banning
Typeset in Bembo by M&S, Toronto

Printed and bound in Canada

McClelland & Stewart Inc.
The Canadian Publishers
481 University Avenue
Toronto, Ontario
M5G 2E9

3 4 5 6 7   04 03 02 01 00

"TOASTED BUNS!"

Travis Lindsay could only shake his head in wonder. The Screech Owls had been in Nagano, Japan, less than an hour, and already Nish was spinning out of control.

"WE GOT TOASTED BUNS!"

The Owls had just checked in to the Olympic Village where they would be staying for the next two weeks. They'd been issued door keys, divided into groups, and assigned to different "apartments" in the large complex that would be home to all the teams competing in this special, once-in-a-lifetime "Junior Olympics." Travis was sharing with Dmitri Yakushev, Lars Johanssen, Andy Higgins, Fahd Noorizadeh – and, of course, his so-called, perhaps soon to be *former*, best friend Wayne Nishikawa.

"COME AND GET YOUR BUNS TOASTED!"

Rarely had Travis seen Nish this wound up. Travis and the other players had been carefully hanging up their clothes or putting them neatly in drawers, when Nish, as usual, had simply stepped into the bedroom he'd be sharing with

Travis, unzipped his bag, turned it upside down, and let shirts and pants tumble into a heap beside his bed. Then he'd gone "exploring."

It took him less than a minute to find out that Japan was the land of the heated toilet seat.

"*Fan-tas-tic!*" Nish had shouted out in triumph. "*At least one country still believes in the electric chair!*"

The rooms were not very warm. The elevator and the stairs were all on the outside of the building, the wind-blown snow powder dancing around the walkways as the Owls had made their way to their little apartments. The apartments were heated, but still cool compared to homes in North America. Each bathroom had its own heater, and the toilet seat itself was wired for heat, with a small red dial on the side to control the temperature. Nish had instantly cranked theirs up as high as it would go.

"THIS IS BETTER THAN WEDGIES!" he had screamed before heading out to crank up all the other toilet seats before anyone else discovered this little miracle of technology.

Travis just shook his head.

He still had unpacking to do. And after eighteen hours of flying, and six hours sitting in a bus as it climbed up from Tokyo into the snow-capped mountains that surrounded Nagano, he was exhausted. His own bed back home couldn't have looked more inviting than this tiny bed with the crisp sheets folded back, waiting for him.

Travis was so tired that not even the screaming and shouting from the other apartments was going to stop him from slipping in between those covers for a quick nap.

"YOU'RE GONNA DIE FOR THIS, NISH!"

That was Sarah Cuthbertson's voice. And if anybody could get revenge on Nish, it would be Sarah.

The Screech Owls had come to Nagano through a remarkable series of coincidences. Several years earlier, their small town of Tamarack had "twinned" with Nagano, which considered itself small by Japanese standards, even though it had close to a hundred times as many people as there were in Tamarack. But "twinning" had been popular at the time, and centres throughout Japan had been approaching North American towns and cities and setting up exchanges. Nagano and Tamarack were both tourist centres. Both had long and snowy winters. Both had ski hills within easy reach. Both were surrounded by bush, but farther from the city, Nagano's bush became mountains, whereas Tamarack's bush just became more bush.

There had been exchanges in the past between the two towns. One of the Tamarack service clubs had gone to Nagano several years back, and a Nagano high-school band had come to Tamarack and put on a wonderful concert at the town hall – but in the past few years, as Nagano had prepared to host the Olympics, there had been no contact.

Now, with the Winter Games over, the town of Nagano had sent out the most surprising invitation: Would there be a hockey team in Tamarack that would like to come over and play in Big Hat? Big Hat, of course, was the main arena at the Olympic Games. It was here that Dominik Hasek of the Czech Republic team had stopped five players from Team Canada, one after the other – Theoren Fleury, Raymond Bourque, Eric Lindros, Joe Nieuwendyk, Brendan Shanahan – in that amazing shootout that had eliminated Canada. And it was here that the brilliant Hasek had then shut out the mighty Russians. In a single season, Hasek had won the Olympic gold medal and, four months later, been named, for the second year in a row, the most valuable player in the National Hockey League.

But now that the Games were over, the city of Nagano had decided to turn Big Hat into a huge gymnasium. It would never again serve as a hockey rink.

There would, however, be one last gasp. The head of Japanese hockey, Mr. Shoichi "Sho" Fujiwara, had talked the city of Nagano into putting on one final tournament at Big Hat. He had even received approval from the International Olympic Committee to use the official Olympic symbol and call this once-in-a-lifetime tournament the "Junior Olympics." It would feature Japan's future Olympic stars, or so hoped the organizers. The best peewee teams in Japan were invited. A team was invited from Lake Placid, New York, where the Winter Olympics had been held nearly twenty years earlier, and an invitation had gone out, as well, to the Canadian town of Tamarack.

Both Lake Placid and Tamarack readily agreed. Not every Owl was able to go, of course. Jeremy Weathers, their No. 1 goaltender, had a family vacation booked to Disney World and wouldn't be able to make it. But Jenny Staples, the backup, was more than up to the challenge. And for once the fundraising was not left up entirely to the Owls and their families. The service club was pitching in with a new wheelchair and enough money to cover the cost of Data going along as a special "assistant coach." The local radio station was putting up some money. The town council voted five thousand dollars toward the exchange. A Canadian airline, as a goodwill gesture and to promote its own links with Japan, offered free passage for the players and coaches.

What seemed like a financial impossibility one week, was a certainty the next: the Screech Owls were off to Nagano!

No one, of course, took the trip as seriously as Nish. He called the visit his "homecoming" – ignoring the fact that his great grandfather, Yasuo Nishikawa, had left Japan for Canada a whole century earlier. Nish, who had once proudly claimed he didn't know a single word of Japanese and didn't care, was suddenly the self-proclaimed expert on the Land of the Heated Toilet Seat.

He had been insufferable since the plane had taken off – and not just because he twice tried to "stink out" the section where the Owls were attempting to catch some sleep. Nish was so excited, he didn't fall asleep until just before the plane landed. And now, while everyone else seemed to be having trouble dealing with the jet lag – the dizzying effect of convincing your body that it hadn't missed a night of sleep – Nish was running ahead of them all, as if he had somehow picked up the energy they had lost.

He acted like he knew everything. Back home he'd called up his grandfather to get some Japanese sayings, and was shouting "*Moshi moshi!*" to everyone he bumped into.

"It means 'Hello,'" he explained to Travis, as if

Travis was some infant who had never heard the spoken word before.

"'*Arigato*' means 'Thank you.'"

"Thank you," said Travis with some sarcasm.

"*Arigato*," said Nish, entirely missing Travis's point.

He told everybody to be careful with their shoes. "You can't walk into a house or restaurant with your shoes on," he said. "You have to have slippers."

Nish turned out to be right about the shoes, which rather impressed some of the other Owls. As they found their rooms in the Olympic Village, they discovered small blue slippers waiting for them at the entrances. The slippers slid on easily, and almost instantly the Owls had taken to skating about the small apartments, the new footwear sliding effortlessly on the highly polished floors.

That first evening, after Travis had taken his little nap, and Nish had practically electrocuted the entire building, the Owls gathered with the other teams in the large tent that had been erected between the buildings and which would be their gathering place for meals and relaxation for the remainder of their stay. Tonight was to be the opening banquet, with the mayor of Nagano and other area dignitaries welcoming the teams to the first-ever, and probably only-ever, Junior Olympic Hockey Tournament.

Muck Munro, the Owls' coach, had laid down the law. Dark pants, no jeans. White blouse or shirt and tie. Team jacket. "You're not here just representing your town," he told them. "You're here representing your country."

That seemed to upset Nish's plans. He had told Fahd he was headed out to find a store where he could buy a package of adult diapers. He told Fahd – and Fahd, of course, had believed him – that he was going to go to the banquet as a sumo wrestler, his big stomach hanging out over the diaper, and that he planned to spend the evening "belly bumping" the players on the other teams.

"I think he needs a straitjacket, not a diaper," said Sarah.

"You should have been sitting next to him on the plane," said Fahd. "He needs a diaper, all right."

Nish was, of course, kidding. But he did go out to explore, and came back about an hour later even more expert on the subject of Japan than he'd already been, if that were possible.

"Japan," he announced, "is the most civilized country on Earth. If you can't find what you want in a vending machine, it doesn't exist."

To prove his point, he began laying out his vending-machine loot on the bed, pulling treasures from his jacket pocket as if they were stolen jewels and the rest of the Owls were his accomplices gathered in some back alley.

"Cigarettes," he announced, dropping two packages down on the bed.

"You're not old enough to buy smokes!" Fahd protested.

Nish shrugged a world-weary shrug and yanked something from his other pocket. A can, and a small bottle.

"Beer," he announced. "And whisky."

"*Where'd you get this?*" Fahd almost screeched.

"Vending machines. Anybody can use them. You just put your yen in and push any button you want."

"You don't even smoke!" said Sarah, disgusted.

"And you *certainly* don't drink!" said Fahd, still alarmed.

"You just watch what the ol' Nisher drinks," Nish announced, reaching into an inside pocket of his jacket.

He pulled out a tall blue can. On the side was one word in large white letters: *Sweat*.

Nish held out his can of "Sweat," smacked his lips, pulled the tab, and hoisted the drink high, guzzling it down until he'd finished half the can.

He pulled the drink away, burped loudly, and held it out, his eyes having taken on their most kindly look.

"A slug of Sweat, anyone?"

"*I think I'm gonna hurl!*" yelled Fahd.

Nish tossed the drink to Travis, who caught the skinny blue can before it spilled onto the

9

floor. He held it up to his nose and sniffed quickly. It didn't *smell* like sweat. The idea that anyone would produce a drink that would taste like the inside of a hockey bag was a bit much for Travis to believe, and he sniffed again. It smelled almost sweet. He glanced at the writing on the side. Most was in Japanese, but there was also some English: "Pocari Sweat is highly recommended as a beverage for such activities as sports."

He took a taste: sweet fizzy water. Nice. Perhaps it was just a misspelling: "Sweat" instead of "Sweet."

"It's okay!" said Travis.

"What do you say?" Nish announced grandly. "Do the Screech Owls have a new team drink?"

"Sounds good to me," Travis said, passing on the can of Sweat so others could try a sip of the sweet, cool liquid.

Nish was in his glory. The Owls were hanging on his every word. Phoney or not, he had established himself as the Owls' expert on Japan.

"Muck says we gotta look nice," Nish announced next. "But we gotta act right, too. You meet people here, you don't shake their hands, okay – you *bow*."

To demonstrate, he stood back, set his heels together, and made a deep bow to Sarah, who giggled and bowed back.

"No handshakes," Nish barked. "*Bow.* You got it? *Bow.*"

"What about high-fives?" Wilson asked. "What do we do when we score?"

"What you always do," Nish said with a wicked grin. "Shout *'Way to go, Nish!'*"

2

MUCK WOULD BE PLEASED, TRAVIS KNEW, AS THE Screech Owls assembled by the entrance to the tent and awaited the arrival of their coach. Travis had taken special care in combing his hair. He had moved the blond curl back off his forehead. It made him look older, he thought, more mature. More like a team captain.

They were all there. Wilson and Andy the tallest, by far. Gordie Griffith still managing to look like a little boy and a skinny teenager at the same time. Sarah with her blonde hair in a neat ponytail. Jenny with her flame-red hair shining like it had sparkles in it. Dmitri with his hair slicked down, and Lars with his hair so light and dry it seemed like it might bounce off his head just from walking. And Nish, of course, wearing his beloved Mighty Ducks of Anaheim cap.

"You hoping they'll mistake you for Paul Kariya?" Sarah kidded.

"Very funny," Nish said, but refused to remove the cap. Travis understood why. It had, after all, been given to Nish by Paul Kariya at the end of the Quebec International Peewee

Tournament, and Nish had hardly taken if off since. It was, for him, the symbol of his greatest moment on the ice – he'd scored the winning goal – and his greatest moment *off* the ice, as well. He had met his great hero, Paul Kariya. And Kariya had forgiven Nish for letting on that they were "cousins" just because they were both of Japanese heritage.

Muck came along with Mr. Dillinger, the team manager, and Mr. Dillinger was pushing Data in his fancy new wheelchair. Data looked great. His dark hair was combed perfectly and he had put on his new blazer with the Screech Owls logo over the heart. It was amazing what Data could do with a single hand: loop a tie, button his cuffs, tie his shoes, practically anything that anyone else could do with two. Data, the electronics nut, had a video camera small enough to hold in his one good hand, and was using it to sweep the scene, lingering on each player as he recorded their first day in Nagano.

Both Muck and Mr. Dillinger were in suits, but Mr. Dillinger, his happy red face grinning, his bald head shining, looked far more at ease in his fancy clothes than did Muck. Muck kept pulling at his collar, and he kept scratching the top of his legs as if the pants itched him. But if Muck didn't much care for how he was dressed, he seemed to like what he saw in his team. His only adjustment was to pluck the Mighty Ducks cap off Nish and slam it into his stomach before announcing it was time to go in to the opening banquet.

The Owls were put at the same table as the Olympians, the peewee team from Lake Placid. The Olympians were wearing beautiful red-white-and-blue tracksuits, the U.S. flag emblazoned across the back with the Olympic symbol and "1980" stitched on beneath. The Owls knew that 1980 was pretty much a sacred year in Lake Placid – the year the home team, the United States, had won the Olympic gold medal.

There were more than a dozen teams crammed into the tent. There were the two teams from North America, at least ten from Japan, and even two from China, where hockey was just beginning to be played.

The teams were shy of each other, but gradually they began to mingle as they were prodded by their coaches and the tournament organizers. Nish made a great show of bowing to various members of the Japanese teams, who giggled shyly into their hands and bowed back. The Japanese all seemed to have their own cards – kid versions of the business cards Travis's dad sometimes gave out – and Nish seemed to be the only North American player there with cards to hand back: hockey cards of NHL stars, usually, but also a few of his treasured "Wayne Nishikawa" cards from the Quebec International Peewee Tournament. Nish was a huge hit, with his Japanese looks and his treasured Mighty Ducks cap, which was now back on his head. One by one, Japanese players lined up to try on the cap that had been given to Nish "by the great Paul Kariya himself – my *cousin*."

Muck and Mr. Dillinger were invited to the head table. Sho Fujiwara, recognizing a hockey man like himself in Muck, did a quick switch of the place cards that indicated the seating arrangements so that they could sit together and talk – and Muck seemed to be having a wonderful time of it in this strange, foreign country where his game served as the common language. At one point, Travis even noticed Muck showing Sho a break-out pattern by using the water glasses and salt and pepper shakers to illustrate the Owls' game plan.

Sho opened the ceremonies with a hilarious account of his own experiences as the Japanese goaltender for the 1960 Winter Olympics in Squaw Valley, California. In Japanese, and then English, he told the kids what it was like to be on the very first hockey team that ever played for Japan, and the pressure they were under. They sailed across the Pacific rather than flew, so they'd have time to work on new skills on the way across. "Not stickhandling," he said with a wide smile, "but learning how to eat with a knife and fork."

He soon had the kids screaming with laughter. Each member of the Japanese team had been issued an official Japanese Olympic team shirt and tie for the trip, and they had worn them each day aboard the ship as it had made its way across the ocean, practising three meals a day to do without the traditional chopsticks and eat with the knives and forks they would be expected to use in North America. "We landed in Vancouver," he said. "First thing we all did was go out and buy a new shirt and tie each. Our official ones we had to throw away, we'd spilled so much food on them!"

Sho then introduced the head table. Besides Muck and Mr. Dillinger and the head of the Lake Placid and the Chinese teams, the mayor of Nagano was present, as was the head of the service club from Tamarack, the head of the local sports federation, and a few local businessmen, including Mr. Ikura, the man who owned the largest of the nearby ski resorts, who stood to extend an invitation to all the teams to come to his hill for a day of skiing and snowboarding – "free of charge" – before the end of the tournament. He was, of course, cheered wildly.

After the introductions, they served the food. Nish insisted he was going to eat his with chopsticks, and made a grand gesture of getting his sticks ready and pushing away the knife and fork that had also been laid out at his plate.

"What's *this*?" demanded the Japanese expert as the first plate was placed in front of the Owls.

"Sushi," announced Sarah.

"I thought you'd have known all about sushi, Nish," said Jenny.

"What *is* it?" snarled Nish. "It looks alive!"

"It's raw," said Sarah. "Raw fish."

"Whatdya mean? They cook it at our table, like that steak they do in restaurants?"

"You eat it raw," said Jenny.

"I'm not eating anything that hasn't been cooked!"

Travis looked at the plates as they landed in front of him. The sushi looked more like artwork than food. It was beautiful, each piece perfectly laid out on a little roll of rice with small, green sprigs of vegetable around it. On each roll of rice there was a slice of fish, some very pale, some very red, and some, it seemed, with tentacles.

"Is that what I think it is?" Travis asked Sarah. Sarah followed his finger.

"It's octopus," she said. "Raw octopus."

Jenny, who seemed to know a great deal about sushi, took over. Like a patient teacher, she pointed to each piece of sushi laid out on the plates before them.

"This one is eel."

"*Yuuucckkkk!*" said Nish.

"Squid."

"*Yuuucckkkk!*"

"Raw eggs."

"*Yuuucckkkk!*"

"More octopus tentacle . . ."

But Nish was already up and scrambling. He had his Paul Kariya cap over his face and was bolting for the far exit as fast as he could move. Travis noticed that Data had pulled up near the table in his wheelchair and had recorded the entire scene. Good old Data — they'd want to show *that* one day!

Travis couldn't help laughing. He had seen Nish act like this once before, when the team was visiting the Cree village of Waskaganish and Nish had eaten, without realizing it, some fried "moose nostrils." But Nish had come around eventually, and had eventually eaten, and enjoyed, beaver and goose and even some moose nostril. He would come around here in Japan, too. He had to. He was, after all, Mr. Japan on this trip. And this was Japanese food.

Travis tried the sushi cautiously. Sarah and Jenny and Lars had no concern about it, and ate happily. Travis chose the raw tuna to start — he had tuna sandwiches most days at school — and it wasn't bad. He tried dipping it in the small bowl of soya sauce and green mustard that Jenny held out to him. It tasted even better. He tried the salmon and it was delicious. He tried the octopus, but it was rubbery and made his skin crawl — particularly when he bit down on one of the tentacles — and he spat the rest of it out into his napkin and stayed away from the octopus from then on.

Toward the end of the meal, Sho stood up and

introduced the mayor, who would be making a few welcoming remarks to the teams.

The mayor rose slowly, seeming to bask in the applause from the assembled players.

He was an older man – but even so, Travis thought, he moved slowly.

As he got to his feet, he seemed a bit unsteady.

Concerned, Sho reached for the mayor's elbow.

Muck leapt to his feet and rushed to help, his chair tipping over and clattering onto the floor.

The mayor reached for his throat, then plunged straight forward, his face twisting horribly as he fell across his plate, the legs of the head table giving way under him and the entire table – trays of sushi, flower arrangements, glasses of water, knives, forks, and chopsticks – crashing down onto the floor with him.

Mr. Dillinger, who knew first aid, pushed his way through and reached the mayor. He turned him flat on his back, yanking his collar loose.

He bent down, his ear to the mayor's open, twisted mouth.

He looked up, blinking at Muck and Sho Fujiwara.

"*He's dead!*"

3

SARAH LEANED OVER THE CHAIR IN THE SITTING room, her chin in her hands, her eyes red-rimmed from the shock and strain of the hours since the banquet the night before.

"I've never seen anyone have a heart attack," she said.

"My grandfather had one," said Travis. "But he drove himself to the hospital – it wasn't like this at all."

"He looked like he was being strangled."

There had been no hope for the mayor of Nagano from the moment Mr. Dillinger bent down over him. An ambulance had arrived quickly, and the body had been removed at once, but the shock lingered.

For once, even Nish was quiet. Suddenly electric toilet seats and drinking Sweat didn't seem quite so funny. They hadn't known the mayor of Nagano, none of them had even been introduced to him, but he had been thoughtful enough to come out and welcome them to his city.

They were feeling sorry for the mayor and sorry for themselves when the door opened and

Muck came in. The coach was dressed much more normally now, in an old tracksuit and his team jacket. But he didn't look normal. Muck's face was grey and serious.

"It wasn't a heart attack," he told them.

"What was it?" The question, of course, came from Fahd.

Muck took some time answering. Travis, sitting closest to him, could see his big coach swallow several times. A muscle on the side of Muck's cheek was twitching.

"The police say . . . he was . . . poisoned."

"*Poisoned?*" Travis repeated, hardly believing it.

"How?" Fahd asked again. "We all ate the same meal."

"I told you that sushi stuff was poison," Nish said.

"*Shhhhhh,*" Sarah ordered. This was no time for Nish's stupid humour.

"They found traces of blowfish in his stomach," Muck said.

"*Blowfish?*" Fahd asked. "What the heck's *blowfish?*"

By lunchtime, they all knew everything there was to know about blowfish. Called *fugu* in Japanese, the blowfish is able to inflate its body by swallowing water or air so that it swells into a ball. The Japanese treasure the ugly creature as a great

21

delicacy, and chefs are trained for years in how to clean the fish so that none of the poison that is found in some of its internal organs spreads into the flesh. Even so, about a hundred Japanese a year die accidentally from the deadly poison.

"It wasn't an accident," Muck had told them. "There was no blowfish on the menu. Someone had to deliberately put it on the plate he was served."

"Who would want to do something like that?" Fahd had asked.

"The police have taken the two chefs in for questioning."

Travis's mind was racing. Why would anyone want to kill that nice old man? Travis had no idea. He knew nothing about the mayor, not even his name. And why would they kill him at the hockey banquet? In front of a couple of hundred peewee hockey players?

It suddenly struck Travis: *I am a witness to murder. I have seen one human being killed by another human being. And the way murders are usually solved is by questioning the witnesses.*

What did I see? Travis asked himself. *Nothing. What do I suspect? Nothing.*
What do I know? Nothing.

"There's nothing we can do about it," Muck said after the Owls had discussed the matter at length. "It's unfortunate, and we are all sorry for the mayor's family. Mr. Dillinger is sending our sympathies to them. But the matter is now under investigation by the police – nothing to do with us, nothing to do with this hockey tournament. The best thing we can do is move on."

"Do we know who we're playing yet?" Lars asked.

Muck pulled out a schedule. He opened it, scanning sections he'd already underlined in red ink.

"Our first game is Thursday morning against the Sapporo Mighty Ducks."

"The *Sapporo Mighty Ducks*," Nish said with a sneer. "What a joke!"

"Maybe the rest of your 'cousins' will be on the team," said Sarah.

"Very funny."

"Are they any good?" Travis asked.

"Don't know," Muck said, stuffing his schedule back into his breast pocket. "That's why we need to practise. We're on in an hour – get your stuff. Mr. Dillinger and I have a little surprise worked up for you."

"What?" Fahd asked.

Muck smiled. "If I told you, it wouldn't be a surprise any more, now would it?"

4

TRAVIS WAS GLAD TO GET BACK HOME – BECAUSE that's how he felt on skates, on ice, in his own hockey equipment, surrounded by his own smell, his own teammates, with everything in its place, everything where it should be. His eyes knew where the net would be without even looking. His shoulder had a sense of the boards. His imagination held a thousand different ways to score a goal.

There is something universal about the way a skate blade digs into the first corner on a fresh sheet of ice, Travis thought, as he took his first spin around the Big Hat ice surface. This was the same ice surface where Dominik Hasek had put on the greatest display of goaltending the world had ever seen. But it felt no different than the arena back home. Travis and the Owls had skated on the Olympic rink in Lake Placid, and they had played in the Globen Arena in Stockholm, where the World Championships had been played – but the sound of his blade as it cut through that first corner was the same as in Lake Placid, in Sweden, the same, for that matter, as on the frozen creek where they sometimes played at the edge of town back home.

On skates, Travis had a different sense of his body. He felt bigger, because of his pads. Stronger, because of his skills. Faster, because his body was pumping with so much pent-up emotion that he felt he *needed* to play almost as much as he *wanted* to. Now that he was on the ice, everything felt right: Sarah was sizzling on her skates just ahead of him, Nish puffing back of him as they went through their wind sprints, Dmitri's skates barely touching the ice surface as he danced around the first and second turns, Lars striding low and wide, the European way.

Everything was right here. Murder did not exist here.

Even Muck's whistle felt right: music from centre ice. Travis and Sarah cut fast around the far net and headed for the coach, the two of them coming to a stop in a fine spray of ice. The other Owls came in spraying as well, Muck waiting, whistle to mouth, until the last of them – Nish, naturally – came spinning in on his gloves and shinpads, the toes of his skates looping odd circles in the ice behind him.

Travis had raced to centre so automatically that he hadn't even looked up. He hadn't noticed that Muck was not alone.

"This, here, is Mr. Imoo," Muck said, indicating the little man beside him. "He's a Buddhist priest, so show him proper respect. He also knows his Japanese hockey."

The Owls stared in wonder. If this was a priest, none of them had ever met another one like him. Mr. Imoo was grinning ear to ear; but his front teeth were missing, top and bottom! He was wearing hockey equipment, but the socks were torn and there seemed to be old dried blood on his sweater.

"Mr. Imoo runs the local hockey club, the Polar Stars – but he's also a priest at the Zenkoji Temple, which you'll be touring later this week. Mr. Dillinger met him at the temple and asked Mr. Imoo if he'd mind coming out to practise with us."

"It is great honour," Mr. Imoo said, bowing deeply towards the Owls.

Nish, who was on his skates now, immediately bowed back, even deeper, causing Mr. Imoo to laugh.

"I see you already have Japanese player," he said.

"Half Japanese," Nish corrected.

"Half *nuts*," Sarah added.

"*Moshi moshi*," said Nish, ignoring Sarah.

"*Moshi moshi*," Mr. Imoo said back.

"I thought Buddhists were non-violent," said Fahd.

"Not the hockey-playing Buddhists," said Mr. Imoo, smiling. "But there's only one of them, me. I lost my top teeth in that corner over there. Keep an eye out for them, please."

The Owls laughed, knowing the teeth would have long been swept up by the Zamboni, if, in fact, the story were even true — which they figured it was, given how fierce Mr. Imoo looked in his ragged hockey gear.

"Mr. Imoo is going to give you the secrets of playing hockey in Japan," said Muck.

"Buddhist secrets," Mr. Imoo grinned. "Very special secrets, only for Screech Owls."

"Listen to what he says," said Muck. "And remember it tomorrow."

"The secret to Japanese hockey is to shoot," Mr. Imoo said.

"That's no secret," Fahd insisted. "Even Don Cherry knows that."

"But in Japan is different," said Mr. Imoo. "Japanese hockey very, very different from North American hockey."

By the time Mr. Imoo was through explaining, the place in Travis's brain that held his hockey knowledge felt as if it had been invaded by an alien force. It made absolutely no sense — hockey sense, anyway.

Japan, Mr. Imoo explained, is a very formal place. Younger people, for instance, are always expected to step aside for their elders, and it applies as well to hockey. On his team, there are *koohai* players — the younger ones, the rookies —

and the older players are called *sempai*. The *sempai* rule the dressing room. The older players sit together, talk together, and bark out orders to the younger *koohai* players.

"*Koohai* have to tape the *sempai* sticks," said Mr. Imoo, "have to get them drinks when they want them — even have to wash their dirty underwear!"

"Seems sensible to me," said Nish.

It would, thought Travis — Nish was the oldest player on the team.

"At least that way your long underwear would finally get cleaned," Sarah said.

But Nish wasn't listening. He seemed hypnotized by Mr. Imoo. He had moved up close and was standing next to him, nodding at everything the Buddhist priest told them.

"Japanese hockey is trying to change this," said Mr. Imoo, "but it is very, very difficult to change old habits. On the ice, the younger *koohai* will never take a shot — they always pass to a *sempai* to take the shot."

"Good idea," agreed Nish.

Mr. Imoo grinned. "This has major effect in hockey. Goaltenders check to see which player is older player and wait for him to get the pass for the shot. Don't have to worry about younger players."

"I like that," said Jenny, the goaltender.

"Goalies also not good in Japan," said Mr. Imoo. "Everyone is afraid of hurting goalie in practice, so no one shoots – not even *sempai*. So goalies not get good through practice. That's why I say secret against Japanese hockey is to shoot puck. Shoot puck, score goal – simple, eh?"

"Yes!" shouted Nish, banging his stick on the ice. Several of the other Owls followed suit. Mr. Imoo grinned widely, the big gap of his missing teeth making his grin all the more infectious.

"You must play like *samurai* – great Japanese warriors, afraid of nothing, attacking all the time. Okay?"

"O-kay!" Nish shouted, banging his stick again.

Muck stepped back into the centre of the gathering. "We're just going to scrimmage. But I want to see shots, okay? Lots and lots and lots of shots. I want quick shots, surprise shots, any shots you can get off, understand?"

"You bet, coach!" Nish said, slamming his stick again. Muck winced. He didn't care to be called "coach." He said that was what American football players called their coach. Canadian hockey coaches, he always said, went by their real names.

"I need a volunteer for goal," said Muck. "We've only got Jenny here. We need another for the scrimmage."

"You got one right here!" said Nish, whose enthusiasm seemed to have gotten the best of him.

As one, the entire team turned and stared at Nish, who was about to bang his stick again on the ice, but now was beginning to blush beet-red. "Why not?" he said.

"You said shoot, didn't you?" Sarah said to Mr. Imoo.

"That's right, *shoot.*"

"Hard?"

Mr. Imoo smiled, realizing the play that went on between Sarah and Nish.

"Hard as you can."

Travis often wondered if other athletes loved their particular games as much as hockey players loved theirs. Did baseball players enjoy practice? Did the Blue Jays or the Yankees ever play a little "scrub" baseball or "knocking out flies" while they were waiting around to play a real game? Did the Pittsburgh Steelers ever play a little "touch football" while gearing up for the Super Bowl?

He doubted it. But hockey players were different. Hockey players *loved* to play a dozen silly little games. Scrimmage, like this, was best of all – a time when you could try any play you wanted, a time when mistakes counted for nothing and no one even bothered to keep score. But there were also contests to see who could hit the crossbar, who could score the most one-on-one, who could hang on to the puck longest, who could pick a puck up off the ice using only the blade of the stick, who could bounce a puck longest on the stick blade, who could bat a puck out of the air best . . .

Scrimmage was when Travis's line shone. Sarah at centre, Travis on left, the speedy Dmitri on right wing. Sarah the playmaker, Travis the checker, Dmitri the finisher.

Sarah made certain they lined up on Jenny's side – with Nish, wobbling in thick pads, his head covered by a borrowed mask, heading for the far net. Mr. Imoo, laughing, skated beside him. The two seemed to have struck up a special friendship – or perhaps Mr. Imoo, like everyone else, was merely amused by Nish's wild antics.

And Nish, of course, was making the most of it. Pretending he was Patrick Roy, he started talking to his goal posts, patting each one as if it were a guard dog that was there to help him out. He lay on his back and stretched like Dominik Hasek. He sprayed the water bottle directly into his face. He charged to the left corner and smashed his stick into the glass before returning to the crease, daring anyone to try to score on him.

Wayne Nishikawa, *samurai* goaltender.

Muck let them play. No instructions. No whistles. He simply let them do what they wanted, watching as they got a feel for the larger ice surface, and watching Mr. Imoo as he scrambled around on his skates and shouted at the players to "*Shoot!*" almost as soon as they got the puck.

Sarah picked up the puck behind Jenny and broke straight up through centre, Dmitri cutting away from her on the right. The moment Gordie Griffith made a move toward her, Sarah flipped the puck to Dmitri, who broke hard down the boards before firing a hard cross-ice pass to Travis.

Travis was ready to shoot, but couldn't resist his little back pass to Sarah. Muck hated the move; Travis loved it. When it worked, it looked brilliant; when it didn't work, it usually meant a breakaway for the other team. But this was scrimmage, so he tried it.

Sarah was expecting the trick pass and already had her stick raised to one-time a slapshot. The puck came perfectly at her, and she put all her strength into the shot, trying to drive it right through Nish if necessary.

The shot was high and hard.

It clipped off Nish's skate blade, smashing against the glass behind the net!

Travis heard three sounds. The puck hitting the glass. Sarah's scream of surprise. And Nish's hysterical laugh.

Travis hadn't even looked at the goal. He did now, and saw Nish lying flat on his back, head sticking up the ice, the heavy pads crossed casually and the skates resting high up one post near the crossbar.

"*Save by Hasek!*" Nish shouted.

He did it all practice long. He sat on the net, his legs dangling, and made saves. He lay on his side on the ice, head resting on his glove hand, and made saves kicking his legs high. He wandered out of the crease and dived back whenever one of the Owls fired a shot at his net, timing his slide just perfectly.

Whatever Nish was up to, it was working.

How it worked, Travis had no idea. Luck? The Japanese gods? Buddha? Or just Nish, trying, and accomplishing, the impossible. Mr. Imoo had tears in his eyes from laughing.

"No one on Earth plays hockey like you!" Mr. Imoo shouted at Nish.

"No one on Earth does anything like him," Sarah corrected.

"He is true *samurai!*" Mr. Imoo pronounced.

Muck blew his whistle long and hard at centre. The Owls skated over to Muck, Nish last, as always, and falling to his pads as he arrived.

"I saw some things I liked," Muck said. "And I saw some things I didn't like."

He turned his gaze on Nish, who had his goalie mask off and was smiling up at Muck, blinking innocently.

"Tournament rules require us to have two goaltenders," Muck says. "You just won yourself a job, Mr. Nishikawa."

Nish's eyes stopped blinking. They opened wider in shock.

His mouth opened as well.

And for once, no sound came out.

5

IN THE EVENING, THE SCREECH OWLS WENT down into the heart of downtown Nagano. It had been Mr. Dillinger's idea, and it turned out to be a good one. It stopped the Owls from thinking about the murder.

Data brought along his video camera, and Mr. Dillinger and Travis and Sarah took turns pushing Data's wheelchair along so that Data could use his good hand to record the scene for when they all got back home.

Travis had never seen anything like this unfamiliar city. What struck him was not so much the people moving everywhere, the cars and the buses and the policemen's whistles at the intersections, it was the powdery snow falling to earth through the brilliant lights, the still-busy stores, and the million different things for sale in packaging so strange that Travis often didn't know whether they were to be worn or eaten. It was like some wild combination of the Santa Claus parade, Disney World, the Eaton Centre in Toronto, Niagara Falls – and a world Travis had never even imagined.

Nish, of course, was acting as their tour guide – even though he himself had not yet been downtown. But obviously he had been quizzing his new pal, Mr. Imoo. He knew there was a McDonald's at Central Square. He knew how to work the vending machines so the team could get cans of Sweat, the new team drink. He knew that the area was renowned for its huge, delicious apples, still looking fresh at the end of the winter. He knew that the main street was called Chuo, that the main department store was halfway up it, and that the Buddhist temple, where Mr. Imoo was a priest and where they would be touring on Saturday, was at the far end. When they crossed at one of the busy intersections, they could see up to the temple in the distance, like some fantastic fairytale setting in the light falling snow and the magical glow of the downtown lights.

Nish, however, didn't know everything.

"What're they wearing?" Fahd had asked, pointing at some shoppers.

Travis had seen others like them before. Every once in a while they would come across someone on a bus or in the street wearing a curious white gauze mask across the mouth and hooked by elastic over the ears. They looked like doctors and nurses about to head into the operating room.

Mr. Dillinger knew. "Health masks," he said. "People with breathing problems wear them when the smog gets bad. A city like this traps smog between the mountains. The masks cut out the pollution."

"We should get them for Nish," Sarah said.

Nish, who had only partially been paying attention, turned around. "What's *that* supposed to mean?"

"Think about it, Stinky."

Nish let the comment pass. His mind was apparently on more important things. From the moment Muck had named him backup goaltender for the game against Sapporo, he had taken his new role to heart.

"Great goaltenders," he had announced to the boys sharing their little apartment, "are nuttier than fruitcakes. You have to be eccentric to play goal."

He had gone down the list of great goalies as if counting off points for an exam. Jacques Plante, who used to knit his own underwear. Glenn Hall, who used to throw up before every game and between periods. Patrick Roy, who talks to goal posts and insists on stepping over the lines in the ice rather than skating over them. Goalies who have secret messages painted on their masks. Goalies who talk to themselves throughout the game, as if they're not only playing but also doing the play-by-play.

"Mr. Imoo's going to help me," Nish announced as they walked along. "He's going to work with me until I'm the first goalie in history to have a force shield."

"A *what*?" Travis had asked.

"He's an expert in martial arts, too – not just a Buddhist priest. He's the greatest guy I ever met. He's got a black belt in judo and he knows tae kwon do, and he's going to teach me how to do the Indonesian 'force shield.' It's a little-known Asian secret that'll give me superhuman powers."

"You already have superhuman power," said Sarah. "Unfortunately, it's in your butt."

"Back off," Nish said. "Look at what I got here."

Nish flattened out a piece of carefully folded paper.

"This is the address of a restaurant where a friend of Mr. Imoo's can bend spoons."

"What's so hard about that?" Jenny asked.

"He doesn't touch them, that's what's so hard about that."

According to Nish, the restaurant was located in what seemed to Travis to be a back alley. It was a narrow passage leading off the main street, not even wide enough for a car to get down. They walked along, Travis growing nervous, until finally Nish stopped and pointed at what looked like little more than a run-down house.

"This is it."

"Your Mr. Imoo's pulling your leg," said Sarah.

"Ha!" snorted Nish. "Let's go."

Nish pulled the front door open and stepped inside. Fahd followed, then Andy, then the rest of them. Travis had to turn Data's chair around and back him up over a small step, but he managed it easily.

Sure enough, it was a tiny restaurant, with barely enough room to hold them all.

A woman came out from behind the cash register clapping her hands together and smiling. Obviously, she was expecting them. She began speaking – very fast and in Japanese – to Nish, who kept bowing and saying, "*Moshi moshi!*" to her, which only made her smile all the more.

She called back into the kitchen and a man wearing a white apron came out, also smiling and bowing. Nish held out his piece of paper. The man took it, nodding as he wiped his hands on the front of his apron, and laughed when he realized why the kids were really there. He had business cards for them all – but in Japanese, of course, so Travis had no idea what they said.

Travis was shocked at the reception. Back home, he thought, kids like him and Nish and Sarah were often regarded with suspicion the moment they walked into a store or a restaurant on their own. Often, they couldn't get anyone to wait on them. They got ignored in lines. It was as if somehow, at the age of twelve or thirteen, they'd just broken out of prison, where they were serving life sentences for shoplifting and armed holdups.

But not here. Not in Japan. There was such trust, such open acceptance, even if they were just kids. The woman had an Olympic pin for each of them. Sarah, luckily, had a small Screech Owls crest to give her in return. A man who had been sipping a large bowl of soup picked up and moved off happily to give the Owls and the restaurant owner more space at the one large table in the place.

Just then, the door of the restaurant opened again. It was Mr. Imoo, his ragged hockey bag over his shoulder, a stick in one hand, and a huge Band-Aid over his nose that oozed with fresh blood.

Nish seemed ecstatic to see his new hero, racing to help Mr. Imoo unload his hockey gear.

"What happened to you?" Nish asked.

"Good hockey game tonight," Mr. Imoo grinned.

"Who won?" Fahd asked.

Mr. Imoo grinned again. "Game or fight?"

Mr. Imoo seemed particularly pleased with his little joke. He explained it, in Japanese, to the restaurant, tapping his injured nose a couple of times while everyone else laughed and giggled. Whatever Mr. Imoo was, thought Travis, he wasn't at all like the minister of the church his family attended back home.

The woman brought over a handful of spoons.

"How come he doesn't use chopsticks?" Fahd asked.

Nish turned to him with a look of astonishment combined with disgust.

"Chopsticks," he informed Fahd, "are made of wood."

"My goodness," said Sarah, "*such* an expert."

Giggling, the man placed one of the spoons in the centre of the table, and then fell very quiet. He seemed to withdraw into his body, his arms folding tightly over his chest. His eyes were closed and he began to rock slightly, as if gathering his energies.

Mr. Imoo, the snow still melting in his hair, also went quiet, not even bothering to wipe away the long drop of melted snow that rolled down one cheek.

The Screech Owls fell silent too, but most of them slyly looked around to catch the eye of a friend, their expressions all asking the same question: *What on earth is going on here?*

But not Nish. Nish was even rocking slightly himself, his eyes almost closed but open just enough that he could keep them on the restaurant owner.

The man grunted once and opened his eyes. He had somehow changed, as if almost hypnotized, and it seemed he was now totally unaware of their presence.

He reached out his index finger. Slowly, carefully, he ran it lightly along the length of the spoon, almost as if he were reaching out to tickle a cat's stomach.

Suddenly his hand moved with astonishing speed, the fingers fanning, and in the blur Travis thought he must have lost sight of the spoon, for when the hand pulled back, the spoon was still there, in the centre of the table – but twisted almost in a perfect circle.

"*Outstanding!*" Nish said, nodding his head rapidly.

"How'd he do that?" Fahd asked.

"It's a trick," Sarah said.

"No trick," Mr. Imoo said.

"Can I film it?" Data asked.

Mr. Imoo spoke quickly, in Japanese, to the man, and the man nodded back in agreement.

"Go ahead," Mr. Imoo said to Data. "This is special one for Sarah."

With Data's camera rolling, the man placed another spoon in the centre of the table, then reached out and gently took Sarah's hand in his. Sarah seemed nervous, and Travis could see that she was blushing, but she let the man guide her hand to the spoon and place her fingers over it to feel that it was made of stainless steel.

He took her hand in his again, and while her hand rested on his, for a second time he ran a finger lightly along the spoon, flicked his fingers once, and another curled spoon lay on the table.

Sarah yanked her hand back as if it had just touched fire.

"Is it hot?" Fahd asked.

"N-no," Sarah stammered. She reached out and carefully picked up the bent spoon.

"For you," the man said, gesturing that Sarah should take it.

"Th-thank you," Sarah said, blushing deeply now. She took the spoon, rolled it once in her hand, and then placed it proudly in her lapel buttonhole.

"*Arigato*," she said to the man. "Thank you."

The restaurant owner got up and bowed deeply. He seemed very pleased that Sarah had thought his spoon worthy of a fashion statement.

"Mr. Imoo's going to teach me how to use the force shield," Nish announced to no one in particular.

"You already bend your stick blades too much," said Lars. Everyone laughed.

"You laugh now," said Nish. "You won't be laughing when ol' Nish starts sending players flying with a flick of his glove."

Mr. Imoo giggled and put a hand gingerly to his battered nose.

"Force shield not protect me tonight, that's for sure."

6

IT WAS THE MORNING THEY WERE TO TRAVEL TO Mount Yakebitai, site of the first-ever Olympic competition in snowboarding. On the way they passed through some of the most spectacular scenery Travis had ever seen, but not all the Owls were interested in looking out into the bright, sunlit day.

"Put on a movie!" Nish had screamed from the back.

"Open a window!" Sarah, sitting directly behind him, screamed a moment later.

Mr. Dillinger went to the front of the bus and tried to arrange with the driver to put a movie on the bus's video system, but the driver, unfortunately, had no movies.

"Shoot," moaned Nish. "I wanted to see *Godzilla* in the original Japanese!"

"Hey, Data!" Sarah called ahead to where two seats had been removed to accommodate Data's chair. "Put on your tape. I want to see how that guy bent those spoons."

"Yeah!" shouted Fahd. "Me too."

Everyone was in agreement, and Mr. Dillinger

set about rigging the machine so it would play what Data had recorded so far of the Screech Owls' great trip to Nagano.

"Where is it?" Mr. Dillinger called back to Data as he began pushing the "rewind" button on the machine.

"Not too far," said Data. "About now!"

Mr. Dillinger pushed the "stop" button, then "start." A picture began dancing, badly out of focus, on the screens throughout the bus.

Mr. Dillinger fiddled with the tracking buttons and the picture came into sharp focus. It was the opening-night banquet.

"Too far!" called several voices up and down the bus.

"*Hey!*" Nish shouted. "*Hold it right there for a second!*"

Mr. Dillinger looked back, startled.

"*Pause it!*" Nish shouted. "*Pause it!*"

Mr. Dillinger hit the "pause" button. Travis looked closely at the screen. There seemed to be nothing of importance on it. Just a waiter carrying a tray of sushi toward the head table.

"It's a mistake," Data said. "I didn't know how to work the camera then."

"*No!*" Nish shouted. "*Back it up a touch!*"

Mr. Dillinger pushed "reverse" and then "play."

"*That's the creep who dumped me!*" Nish shouted, anger in his voice.

Travis turned in his seat, startled. *What was Nish going on about?*

"Whatdya mean?" Fahd called out.

"The night of the banquet. Remember when I left the tent?"

"I remember when you ran out crying like a baby," said Sarah.

"I thought I was gonna hurl, remember?"

Sarah rolled her eyes at Travis. Why did they have to go over all this again?

"So?" Lars said. "*This guy* made you throw up?"

"No-no-no-no. When I was out in the entrance. This guy comes running through like something's chasing him. Bowls me right over."

"Maybe he didn't see you," suggested Fahd.

"He saw me all right. He had to step over me to get past. I see him again, he's dead meat."

"What're you gonna do?" shouted Andy. "Blow him apart with your force shield?"

"Very funny," said Nish. "Very, very funny."

Nish folded his arms over his chest and closed his eyes. Whether he was just shutting out the shots he was taking from his teammates or gathering his forces to bend Andy like a spoon, Travis couldn't tell.

But he could tell that Nish was upset at whatever had happened to him. It did seem odd to Travis. People in Japan were so polite. They seemed always to be apologizing for no reason.

And he had never seen anyone move so fast unless it was on skates.

Why would a waiter be running through that way anyhow? The kitchen was in the other direction, and through revolving doors.

And wasn't this just about the same time that the mayor had stood up and dropped dead from the blowfish?

Fahd asked what everyone else was thinking: "Is the death on the tape?"

"A bit," said Data.

"There's no need for anyone to see that," said Mr. Dillinger, his thumb hard against the "forward" button. "Who wants to see the spoon bend?"

"Me!"

"We do!"

"I do!"

"Me!"

Mr. Dillinger pushed the "play" button and the fuzzy picture cleared to show the little downtown restaurant. The woman was just coming to the table carrying the spoons.

A cheer went up through the bus.

But not from Travis. There was something about what had happened to Nish that was bothering him. Something to do with a man running away from a murder that was just about to happen.

7

IF THERE WERE NO SUCH THING AS THE MAGIC of skating, Travis thought, then he would choose snowboarding as the perfect way to travel through life. If he loved nothing more than the sense of his sharp skates on a new, glistening sheet of ice, he loved almost as much the feeling that came from a sharp carve on a good snowboard.

He liked to get his hands down low, his knees bent, and the carve so deep that his hips all but brushed against the snow as it flew past him. A few quick curves, a jump, a quick tail grab, and a perfect landing, immediately into another hard, hard carve, the snow sizzling beneath the board almost exactly as ice will sometimes sizzle beneath your skates.

Travis was not the best snowboarder, but he was pretty good. Best were Sarah and Lars, who were probably the best technical skaters on the team, and fastest, as usual, was Dmitri. But Fahd wasn't far behind. Fahd, in fact, was a far better snowboarder than skater, and Travis was secretly delighted that his friend now had something to brag about.

Nish was hopeless. Well, not exactly hopeless, but he had no patience, expecting his expertise in hockey to serve him just as well in snowboarding. He also thought — or claimed to think, anyway — that snowboarding should be a contact sport. But Nish felt that way about every game he played. He was convinced that baseball would be more fun if you could tackle the runners.

The Owls had been welcomed to Mount Yakebitai by Mr. Ikura, the owner of the ski resort and, according to Nish's information from Mr. Imoo, the owner of several of the top ski and snowboarding hills in the area. He was reputed to be a very, very wealthy man, and was renowned for his generosity. Of his generosity there was no doubt: he had met the Screech Owls with free passes, free board rentals, and a voucher for each youngster for a full meal at the cafeteria.

"*It's not sushi, is it?*" Nish had whined.

"Anything you want," said Mr. Ikura.

"Dairy Queen Blizzard!" shouted Nish.

"What's that?" Mr. Ikura asked.

"Just ignore him," suggested Sarah. "We all do. And thank you from us all for your kind gift."

Sarah had then presented Mr. Ikura with a team windbreaker, and he had put it on to great cheers from the team. He had thanked them and told them to enjoy their day on the hills.

After his first couple of runs, Travis had come to a smaller hill near the bottom to work with

Nish on his carving. Nish wanted to improve, but seemed willing to allow only his best friend to know how bad he really was.

They were working on Nish's crouch when Mr. Dillinger and Data came along, Mr. Dillinger pushing Data on a special sled. Data was filming again with his camera.

"Put that thing away!" shouted Nish, embarrassed at being caught. "Or else."

"What're you gonna do?" Data laughed. "Use your force shield?"

"I don't want any pictures, okay. Not yet, anyway."

Mr. Dillinger headed back toward the lodge, and Data stayed with the two boys, content to watch without filming, at least for a while. Nish worked hard, sweat covering his face, and Travis was delighted with how quickly Nish's snowboarding was improving. He seemed to have mastered the balancing, and once you had that, you were away.

"Go ahead," Nish told Data with new confidence. "You can take some shots of the master now."

Data picked up his camera and began shooting again. Not just Nish, but the entire hill, the lodge, and a Toyota 4 × 4 that was crawling up the steep road toward them.

The vehicle came to a stop just the other side of some nearby trees. Two men got out and pulled a Yamaha snowmobile from the back, followed by a heavy sled, which they attached to the rear of the snowmobile.

Hill workers, Travis presumed, after a quick glance, but then he noticed Nish was staring fiercely at them.

"The guy in the red coat," Nish said.

"What about him?"

"Isn't that the guy who ran me over?"

Travis looked hard. He had heard the stupid jokes about how all Japanese look the same, and he had heard that there were Japanese jokes about all Westerners looking the same, and he knew that neither was true, but still, he couldn't tell whether this man looked all that much different from any other hill worker he'd seen that day.

"It's the creep, okay," said Nish. "Check the eyebrows."

The eyebrows did stand out. Very dark, and slanted in a V that gave him a slightly mean look.

"Maybe," Travis said.

"No 'maybe' about it. That's him."

"I'll get a shot of him," said Data. "Then we can check it against the other shot."

"I'll take my own shot, thanks," Nish said, bending down.

Nish quickly packed a good hard snowball, reeled back, and let it fly. The snowball flew past the trees separating them and crashed into the side of the snowmobile.

The two men looked up, startled.

Nish shook his fist. "MOSHI MOSHI!" he shouted.

"'Hello, hello'?" Travis translated, puzzled.

Nish grinned sheepishly. "Well, I didn't know what else to say."

The man with the mean eyebrows gave a quick, hard look at the boys and then turned away.

"Got him!" shouted Data.

"Nah!" said Nish. "Missed him."

"No," Data corrected, patting his video camera. "*I* got him."

"That's really going to hurt him," Nish said sarcastically, shaking his head and boarding away, carving like an expert until, leaning too tight into a turn, he fell flat on his face, the snow spraying around him.

"*Got that, too!*" Data shouted triumphantly.

8

TRAVIS CAUGHT UP TO SARAH, DMITRI, LARS, AND Jenny at the top of the gondola run. It was a glorious sight – the sun sparkling on the thick snow, the clouds below them, tucked tight as thick blankets to Mount Yakebitai. It was snowing down there, but at the top, high above everything but the neighbouring bright white mountain-tops, the day was picture perfect. Travis wished Data could get up here with the video camera, but Data had gone back to the lodge and Nish had stayed out on the smaller hill to practise.

They did a long run together, Sarah taking the lead and all the others trying to follow, not only her run but her every move. If Sarah pumped a fist, all five pumped a fist. If Sarah jumped and tucked or did a special grab, everyone did. They dropped down through the clouds and along a high ridge until they noticed some signs indicating danger, and Sarah pulled to a sharp stop in the shelter of some pines. The others pulled in beside her.

"Fun, eh?" Jenny said.

Travis smiled at her. Jenny's face was flushed bright pink. Snow was falling on her cheeks, and melting from the heat as fast as it landed.

Lars was biting into a mittful of powdery snow.

Dmitri was closer to the edge of the pines, staring out over the dangerous slope where no one was to go.

And then the mountain exploded.

Just the roar alone would have terrified Travis. But a moment after the terrible sound hit them, the world began to slip away from under the Owls, and they hit the ground, screaming.

Mount Yakebitai was falling!

"*It's an avalanche!*" Sarah screamed, barely audible over the devastating roar.

"*Hang onto the trees!*" Lars yelled.

Travis rolled to one side, over and over, until he could wrap his arms around one of the pines. The tree was shaking – but holding. Dmitri held on to a pine beside him.

The snow below the Owls seemed to be bucking like a horse. Travis could hear Jenny screeching, but he could also see that she had managed to grab a tree.

He lifted his head higher, the sound almost deafening. He could see out through the pines to the dangerous slope, and he had a sense of being in a moving car.

It felt like he was flying with the trees *up* the hill!

He looked again and realized it was the mountainside slipping down, not him going up. The slope seemed to be sliding like a cloth off a tipped-up table, the roar building and a plume of snow rising thicker than any of the clouds that ringed the mountain.

The roar began to recede, but the ground still shook.

Or is it just me shaking, wondered Travis.

The five Screech Owls lay against the safety of the pine trees until the roar stopped. The sky was still filled with rolling snowflakes when they finally stood, but the avalanche was over. They were still alive.

Jenny was crying. Lars put his arms around her and held her. Travis wished he had enough nerve to do it, but knew he couldn't. He wished he could be that comfortable around other people.

Sarah was creeping to the edge of the pines. Dmitri grabbed her arm.

"Don't!" he said. "There could be a second one any minute."

"Where's it headed?" Sarah asked.

"Toward the lodge," Dmitri answered.

Never had Travis snowboarded so well and so fast – but it meant nothing to him except getting to the bottom of the mountain as quickly as possible. They had to find out if anyone was hurt.

Dmitri went first, body crouched, board singing on the snow. He led them in a high loop away from the avalanche area and into clearer skies that had not yet filled with the burst of powdered snow that had risen like a cloud of smoke from a bomb blast. Sarah followed. Then Travis, Jenny, and Lars bringing up the rear and making sure Jenny was all right.

Travis felt his heart jump when the lodge came into view. *It was safe!* There were skiers and boarders milling about, all staring up toward the practice hill where one edge of the avalanche had rolled over the top like a giant wave.

The five boarders raced down and several of the other Owls, and Muck, came stomping through the snow to greet them. Mr. Dillinger and Data were waving from the deck outside the lodge.

"*You're all right! You're all right!*" Fahd called.

"*We're fine!*" Sarah called back. "*But it was close!*"

"Everyone here okay?" Lars asked.

The others turned to Muck.

Travis looked at the big coach. Maybe it came from running through the cold air, but Muck's eyes were glassy and red around the edges.

"We can't find Nishikawa."

9

THIS TIME, THE FRIGHTENING ROAR CAME FROM inside Travis. He heard Muck's words and instantly the pieces of a terrible picture fell into place: Nish finally figuring out how to snowboard; Nish deciding to work on his carves alone; Nish heading farther up the practice hill to be out of the way until he was ready to show everyone. Nish, smothered by the avalanche.

"NNNNNOOOOOOOO!"

The Owls all turned at once toward the hill where the avalanche had lapped over onto the ski runs. Several trees were broken. Snow was piled up as if ploughs had just cleared the world's largest parking lot. Huge banks of snow had risen out of nowhere, it seemed, the flying powder still in the air and now glittering in the sun that had just broken through.

Already rescue crews were out. Vast snowmobiles like army tanks were rolling out across the hills, and rescue workers in bright-yellow ski jackets were racing toward the trees.

Travis reacted without thinking. He kicked off

his board and began running toward the area where he had last seen Nish.

"*Travis!*" Muck called from behind.

Travis didn't stop. He ran farther and then looked back. The rest of the Owls, Muck included, were following, Muck hobbling over the snow on his bad leg.

The Owls were a team, and a teammate was in trouble.

Travis was sweating heavily now. His heart was pounding, his throat burning. He knew he was half crying but didn't care. Nish was his greatest friend in the world.

He blamed himself for what had happened. He should have stayed with Nish. But Travis had abandoned him to show off with his other friends.

And now Nish was gone.

Travis tried to keep what might have happened out of his head, but couldn't. He could see Nish turning, screaming, and the great wall of sliding snow burying him, crushing him.

Right now, Nish might be trying to scream for help – gagging on snow and slowly losing the fight to stay alive.

The rescue workers were out on the avalanche section now. They were crawling on their hands and knees and pulling behind them thin hollow rods that looked like gigantic long straws. Several of the rescuers were already working with the rods, inserting them into the snow and prodding deep below the surface. If somehow Nish was still alive, he would be able to breathe through one of them until they dug him out!

Travis felt his heart skip with hope. The rescuers obviously felt there was a chance. A million tonnes of snow wasn't like a million tonnes of rocks. Nish might still be alive!

Travis found himself praying. He was crying and praying and creeping along on his hands and knees as if he half expected to see Nish's Screech Owls' tuque sticking out of the snow, or hear his muffled voice complaining about sushi or something.

"What the hell is everybody looking for?" A voice behind him asked.

"*Nish!*" Travis called back impatiently.

"What?" the voice asked stupidly.

"*We're looking for Nish!*" Travis repeated, anger in his voice.

"*What?*" the voice repeated.

And then it struck Travis: *he knew that voice as well as his own!*

Still down on his hands and knees, Travis turned his head.

Nish was standing there, his mouth full and his hand stuck deep in a bag of potato chips.

"What's up?" Nish asked.

"Where did *you* come from?"

"The tuck shop. Look, they got real chips there – just like at home."

Travis stood up, now, and did what only minutes before he'd thought himself incapable of – he hugged Nish.

"*Hey!*" Nish protested. "Back off. You'll crush my chips!"

Now everyone noticed him. The Owls came flying at Nish as if he'd just scored the winning goal in overtime. Even Muck came racing over, his bad leg in pain but his face laughing as he reached into the crush and rubbed a big, snow-covered glove in Nish's face.

"C'mon!" Nish shouted. "You're crushing my chips!"

But no one was listening to him. They piled on, and soon the bag of chips was as flat as if the avalanche itself had rolled over it, Nish's protests growing increasingly muffled as more and more Owls leapt onto the pile.

"It's a miracle," said Mr. Dillinger. "An absolute miracle."

The Owls had gathered just outside the tuck shop at the lodge. Everyone, it seemed, had bought a new bag of chips for Nish, who was in his glory now. Between mouthfuls he held court, as if he had, in fact, been swept away by the avalanche, but was such a superior snow-boarder that he had simply ridden the wave of snow like a surfer to the safety of the tuck shop.

Everyone had been accounted for. Not just every Screech Owl, but all the hundreds of skiers and boarders who had been on the hill that day. Mr. Ikura, the owner — his face drawn with concern — had gone around and apologized to everyone who had been here. As if all this, somehow, had been his fault.

"A miracle," Mr. Dillinger kept saying.

Eventually, word came up the mountain that the roads were once again open. The Screech Owls were tired and cranky and just wanted to get back to their rooms and rest up for the game against Sapporo.

The bus was loaded and warming up when Muck and Mr. Lindsay came back from the area where the rescuers were still investigating the slide. A watch would be kept throughout the night in case there was any more movement.

For the time being, Mount Yakebitai was closed for business.

Travis was sitting close enough to the front of the bus to overhear Muck talking to Mr. Dillinger.

"Apparently they've never had an avalanche at this time of the year before," Muck was saying. "Mr. Ikura says it doesn't make any sense to him."

How could it make sense? thought Travis.

The mayor murdered . . . Now an avalanche . . . What was going on in Nagano?

10

NEVER HAD A HOCKEY GAME FELT SO WELCOME. The Screech Owls had come to Nagano to play in the "Junior Olympics," but to Travis it seemed that hockey had become the furthest thing from anyone's mind. *Murder. An avalanche. Nish almost killed.* It was time to get back to something that made sense to the Owls.

They went by bus to Big Hat. Travis had instantly seen where the large arena got its name – it looked like one of the old hat boxes his mother kept in the attic, only thousands of times bigger. The dressing rooms were huge. The rink was a marvel.

The Sapporo Mighty Ducks, unfortunately, weren't very good. They had about a half dozen excellent skaters, but only one puck-handler, and a very, very weak goaltender.

Sarah had taken Mr. Imoo's advice to shoot a little too much to heart. She fired the puck in right off the opening face-off, which she had won easily with her little trick of plucking the puck out of the air before it landed and sending it back between her own skates. A quick pivot, a shoulder fake to lose the Sapporo centre, and Sarah wound up for a long slapshot that cleared the blueline, bounced once, and went in through the goaltender's five hole.

Next shift, Andy Higgins, who with Nish had the hardest shot on the team, fired a slapper from outside the blueline that stayed in the air all the way and went in over the Sapporo goalie's out-stretched glove.

Owls 2, Mighty Ducks 0.

Several of the Owls were laughing on the bench.

"Next player who shoots from outside the blueline will sit the rest of the game," Muck announced. He did not sound amused.

The message got through immediately. From then on, the Owls were careful not to embarrass the Japanese team. They carried the puck in to the Mighty Ducks' end and made sure they set up a play before shooting, and the Mighty Ducks' goalie gradually began to gather confidence.

Travis found when he was on the bench he was paying more attention to the way the Ducks played than to the Owls. He kept trying to figure out which players were the older ones. And sure enough, it seemed Mr. Imoo had been right: the younger players always gave the puck to the older ones if they had a chance.

Jenny, however, had very few chances. And whatever came her way, she easily blocked.

By the end of the second period, the Owls were up 5–0, with Dmitri scoring on a break-away, Fahd on a tip-in, and Liz on a pretty deke after being set up to the side of the net by Wilson.

The third period was just about to start when Muck made his announcement.

"Nishikawa – you're in."

Nish had been sitting on the end of the bench, practically asleep in the heavy, hot goal-tending equipment. He hadn't expected to play at all. As backup, he'd concluded his job in Japan was to entertain at practice and daydream during games.

"I can't go in," Nish protested. "I'm no goalie."

"Get over the boards before I throw you over them," Muck said.

Nish scrambled to get onto the ice, but his big pads caught as he vaulted the boards and he fell, heavily, to the ice, causing the first huge cheer from the Japanese crowd at Big Hat.

Jenny came off to a lot of backslapping and cheering from the Owls. Muck put a big hand on the back of her neck and squeezed, a small message of congratulations from the coach.

It took Nish about five seconds to get into it. He hopped over the lines on his way to the net. He talked to his goal posts. He sprayed his face with the water bottle. He skated over to the boards and hammered his stick against the glass, returning fast to his crease, where he slammed his stick hard into each pad and set himself, ready for anything.

The Mighty Ducks must have thought the Owls were putting in their *real* goaltender, for Travis could see concern on their faces and hear it in their voices.

Of course, Travis realized. There were no girls on the teams here. They assumed Jenny was the weak player and Nish was the star — especially when he acted like a star.

Whatever it was that the Mighty Ducks were thinking, it changed their style. Instead of holding on to the puck too long and trying to get it to an older player who might get a shot, the Ducks started throwing long shots into the Screech Owls' end.

The first one went wide, Nish dramatically swooping behind the net to clear the puck as if he were Martin Brodeur.

The second one skipped and went in under Nish's stick!

Owls 5, Mighty Ducks 1.

The goal brought the Ducks to life. They began skating harder. Their one good puck-carrier began to challenge the Owls' defence and twice slipped through for good shots. The first hit Nish square on the chest. The second went between his legs.

Owls 5, Mighty Ducks 2.

"Where's his force shield?" asked Sarah, giggling.

Twice more the Ducks scored, and in the final minute they pulled their own goalie to try to tie the game.

Sarah's line was out to stop them, Travis hoping he might finally get a goal, even if it was into the empty net.

But the Sapporo Mighty Ducks had other ideas. They were flying now, and the good puck-carrier beat Travis and then Dmitri before putting a perfect breakaway pass on the stick of one of the Ducks' better skaters.

He split the Owls' defence and came flying in on Nish, who went down too soon.

The Duck fired the puck high toward the open top corner.

Nish, flat on his back, kicked his legs straight up.

The puck clipped off the top of his skate toe and hammered against the glass.

A second later the horn blew. Game over.

Nish was last into the dressing room, his uniform soaked through with sweat, his big pads seemingly made of cement.

"I guess I saved your skins," he announced. "If it wasn't for me, we'd have been lucky to come out of that with a tie."

11

BACK IN THE DRESSING ROOM, TRAVIS WAS FIRST to notice something was wrong. His clothes were hung up in a very strange order. If he had taken off his jacket first, then his shirt, then his pants, they should not be on the peg pants first, then jacket, then shirt. Not unless they'd been taken off and replaced by someone in a hurry.

"How'd *your* clothes get on *my* peg?" Fahd was asking Andy.

This was even more curious. There was no mistaking big Andy's clothes for anything of Fahd's.

"Someone's rifled through my hockey bag," said Lars.

"Mine, too," said Jesse.

They carefully checked through everything, and nothing appeared to have been stolen. Mr. Dillinger apologized, saying it hadn't seemed like they ever locked dressing-room doors in Japan, so he hadn't insisted. But someone had obviously been in the room.

The mystery began to clear, if only slightly, once they got back to the Olympic Village apartments. Travis had the key to their apartment in his left pants pocket – or so he thought. When he dug deep for it, he found nothing.

Travis wasn't alone. Three others couldn't find their keys either.

Whoever had stolen them had known where the Owls were staying and had raced back to the Village before the team arrived. Someone had been inside the little apartments. Drawers were left open and clothes thrown about the rooms.

"Looks like I unpacked for everybody!" said a surprised Nish when he saw what had happened.

No one could figure out what the burglar was after. Money? Clothes? It was hard to figure out, because nothing had been taken.

In the morning, still with no idea why their apartments had been broken into – the Screech Owls set off to visit the Zenkoji Temple. They took the bus down to the train station and walked up Chuo street toward the sacred temple.

Mr. Imoo met them at the front gate. Until he smiled, the Owls might not have recognized him. He was wearing the frock of a Buddhist priest and looked much like any of the other priests hurrying about the entrance to the various temples – except, of course, for the missing teeth.

"You must see all of it," he told them. "Zenkoji is nearly three hundred years old. But even before that, for hundreds of years, this was a place of worship. Come — let me show you a bit."

Mr. Imoo's tour was incredible. He showed them the walkway to the main hall — "There are exactly seven thousand, seven hundred and seventy-seven stones here," he told them. "Good mathematics problem, designing that" — and he showed them the darkened area in the main hall where the sacred image of Buddha is said to be, which only the highest priests are ever allowed to see.

"More important than Stanley Cup!" Mr. Imoo said, laughing.

Travis couldn't figure him out. Here he was, a priest in a church — Travis guessed this Japanese temple was much the same as a North American church — and though it was clear that the hundreds of visitors milling about were deadly serious, Mr. Imoo was forever joking about things. "Buddha likes laughing," he said at one point. "Buddha enjoys good joke same as anyone."

He showed them the huge stone pots where visitors burned incense, the air sickly-sweet with the smell. He showed them a statue of a man where older visitors lined up just to rub their hands over the smooth stone. "Binzuro," Mr. Imoo explained. "Smartest doctor who ever lived. They rub him to feel better. Try it — it works!"

Some of the Owls did rub their hands over the smiling figure, but they could feel nothing. "Because you're young," Mr. Imoo said. "Come back to Nagano when you're old – you'll see it works."

Mr. Imoo had his own chores to do and couldn't stay any longer, but he left them with a tour guide and some maps of the huge temple complex and told them all that there was one thing they really should do if they got the chance.

"You must experience *O-kaidan*," he told them. "Under the main temple is tunnel. You can see people over there lining up for it. It is very dark down there. Sometimes people get frightened. But when you reach the end, you will find the way out. Stick to the right. And feel for the latch to the door. We call it the 'Key to Enlightenment.' I can not explain it to you, but after you have been through it, you will know."

"I'm going right now!" said Nish.

"You certainly need some enlightenment," said Sarah.

"I'm not going down in some stuffy room with him," Fahd said. "Nish'll stink it out."

"*This* is a temple!" Nish barked at him, outraged. "You don't do things like that in a place like this."

"*Hey!*" cheered Sarah. "It's working! Nish finally sees the light!"

"C'mon!" Nish said to Travis.

Travis shook his head. "Maybe later."

Travis moved off quickly. He only had to imagine the dark tunnel underneath the temple and he shuddered. Travis hated enclosed dark spaces. He didn't even like long elevator rides. He'd do whatever he could to avoid going.

Travis moved on toward the souvenir section, where visitors were lining up for incense and postcards and small silk banners with paintings of the temple on them.

Data wheeled up to him, smiling and excited.

"The others are going to push me through," Data told him. "Here, you hang on to the camera. There's no point taking it down into a dark tunnel. Take some shots of the other temples if you get a chance."

Travis nodded. It was a beautiful sunny day. The pines surrounding the temples were bright and dripping with melting snow.

There were pigeons strutting all over the walkway. Hundreds of them. Thousands of them. An old woman was dumping out bags of dried bread, and the sound of hundreds of more pigeons landing was almost deafening. They darkened the sun. They landed on her arms, her shoulders, her head, all around her. People cheered and children danced and cameras were raised to record it all as the old woman, grinning from ear to ear, stood with both arms out and pigeons by the dozen tried to find a roost on her.

Got to get this for Data, Travis thought.

The video camera was easy to work. He simply pointed and pressed a button with his thumb.

Everything seemed smaller through the lens. Smaller, but somehow sharper. A cloud of pigeons would fall, another would rise, and in the centre of the shot the old woman turned as if on a pedestal, her grin almost as wide as her outstretched arms as the pigeons fought for a foothold.

A small child ran out into the middle and spooked the birds, a thousand wings roaring as the pigeons rose as one and headed back toward the trees. The child spun, bewildered at their sudden disappearance. Travis giggled, knowing he had caught a delightful scene on Data's camera.

He raised the camera back toward the old woman and for the first time saw, through the lens, that someone was pointing at him.

It was Eyebrows.

The waiter who had run over Nish.

The man at the ski hill.

12

TRAVIS PAUSED FOR A MOMENT, HIS HEART RISING like a frightened pigeon. There was just no doubt about it. It was Eyebrows. And he was pointing right at Travis.

How does he even recognize me? Travis wondered, the camera still raised to his eye.

But there was no time to figure out how. Eyebrows was scowling and beginning to move around the square in Travis's direction. There was another man with him, and he was headed around the square in the other direction.

There was no time to ask questions. Travis knew he had to get out of there.

He stepped backwards and turned, but there was no exit behind him – only a long walk to another temple, and no visitors there.

His best bet was the crowd. But to get back amongst the people, Travis had to go straight ahead.

The pigeons were landing again by the thousands, the old woman dumping out another large bag of broken bread. The clamouring sound of the birds was enormous. The crowd of tourists was growing.

Travis checked the sides of the small square. Both men had their eyes fixed on him and were circling toward him, sticking to the outer edges of the square so they could skirt around the loose circle of tourists.

Travis had no choice.

Like the small child, he broke straight for the centre. The pigeons exploded, rising in terror, their thousands of wings blurring Travis's view as he raced past the old woman toward the other side.

Some of the people had covered their ears, the sound was so great. Others were making faces at him, as if disgusted that he would be so thoughtless. But there was no time for Travis to stop and explain.

He allowed himself only one backward glance as he headed back toward the main temple area.

Eyebrows was running! And right behind Eyebrows – the other man!

Travis ran flat out now, twisting and turning through the heavy crowds of pilgrims and tourists, pigeons flying, families scattering as the little foreigner in the Screech Owls jacket broke as fast as he could for the front gates, where the largest crowds seemed to be.

Travis's mind was racing too. He couldn't stop and ask for help: who here would speak English?

And he couldn't seem to lose himself in the crowds. His team jacket and his face set him apart from everyone else.

I have to hide! Travis thought. *But where?*

And then it struck him.

The tunnel.

If he could reach the tunnel, he might find the rest of the team there. Or Muck or Mr. Dillinger.

But the tunnel was dark and airless, with thick, heavy walls bearing in on him.

There was nothing for it. He turned just enough to see that the men were gaining, and he knew it was now only a matter of time before one of them reached him. And then what would the people watching do? Help him? Not likely. They'd assume that the men had been chasing Travis to get him to stop running and scaring up the pigeons. He'd never be able to explain. They'd take him away. He had no idea what for, but he knew it would be bad.

Travis flew over the seven thousand, seven hundred and seventy-seven stones heading to the main temple. He slipped through the thickening crowds as if he were on skates, dipping and deking to find an opening. He was now moving faster than his pursuers.

Up to the main temple he flew. At the top of the wooden steps he saw that everywhere in front of him were mats covered with the shoes and boots of people who had gone inside. Knowing he must, he kicked off his boots and ran, in his socks, over the soft spongy matting that led to the rear of the temple.

There were pilgrims there, lining up to head down into the tunnel.

Apologizing, Travis eased his way through. No one seemed to mind very much. They must have thought he was just catching up to his team-mates. Perhaps that meant Nish and Sarah and everyone else were still down there. He hoped so.

A few feet into the tunnel, the dark and silence descended on him like a blanket. There was no sound but for the breathing of others in the tight line working their way along the nearest wall.

Travis tried to breathe deep, and felt his nostrils fighting to seal out a rush of damp straw — the smell of the mats on the tunnel floor.

He couldn't breathe!

His heart was pounding now, slamming against his chest as if it, too, desperately wanted out. His breath was coming fast and jerky, never enough, and he choked.

He reached out and felt for the wall. He tried to remember what they'd been told: *Stick to the right wall, trust in yourself, and you will feel the key.*

Travis lunged against the wall, finding instant comfort in its solidity. He held Data's camera tight with his left hand and felt ahead with his right as he inched along. He thought he might be crying.

He almost dropped the camera, and then it struck him.

The camera!

Data's video camera!

That's what they were after! They hadn't recognized him at all. They saw the Screech Owls jacket – and the camera!

That's what they had been searching for in the dressing room. That was why they had stolen the keys and broken into the apartments. But they hadn't realized that Data had a separate apartment on the ground floor.

Data had recorded something on the camera that they wanted. *But what?* Did Eyebrows have something to do with the murder?

There was Eyebrows at the banquet. And Eyebrows and one of his friends at the ski hill. But what was the connection?

It didn't matter that Travis couldn't figure it out. It was enough to know that the men were after the camera, and he had the camera.

Should he leave it? Just drop it, and let them have it if they could find it here?

No, he couldn't do that. He had a responsibility. If the camera was that important to them, it must be important to the police as well.

Travis tightened his grip on the camera and edged along a little farther.

There were sounds behind him – something rubbing along the wall!

What was it he was supposed to look for in the tunnel?

A key? The Key to Enlightenment?

Travis reached out, praying. He reached out — and then felt it.

A hand. A strong hand — tightening about his arm!

A thousand pigeons seemed to take off in his chest.

He felt himself being yanked back, hard.

"*This way!*"

Travis was choking. *That voice! It wasn't Muck or Mr. Dillinger or any of the Owls!*

Travis couldn't even scream. With the strong hand drawing him along, he slipped and tripped and slid toward the far end of the pitch black tunnel. He was being dragged away.

But the hand didn't hurt him.

There was a sound: wood rubbing on wood, and then something giving.

The light hit him, a thousand flashbulbs in his eyes, a shot right to the head that sent him reeling back, almost falling.

The hand still held him.

"You're okay now," the voice said.

Travis looked but couldn't see. His eyes were overwhelmed with the light. He held his hands over them, and when he looked through the cracks of his fingers, he saw a familiar toothless grin.

Mr. Imoo!

13

MR. IMOO HAD SAVED TRAVIS — *BUT FROM WHAT?* His fear of dark enclosed spaces? Of getting lost forever underneath the temple?

What if Eyebrows had simply wanted to get even for Nish's snowball? But if that was the case, why would he bring another guy along with him? Another mean-looking guy.

Mr. Imoo had only noticed that Travis had headed into the tunnel and was seeming to take a very long time coming out the other end. He hadn't gone down to rescue Travis from any murderers or anything, just to show him the way out. Visitors often panicked and froze in the tunnel, apparently.

"It happens," said Mr. Imoo. "Don't worry about it."

But Travis couldn't stop worrying. What was going on? Had he been right — was it the camera they wanted? And if so, what was in the camera that was so important to them that they'd break into the Owls' residence and then chase Travis into a sacred temple?

When they got back to the Olympic Village, Travis got Sarah and Nish to sit down with him and go through the video cassette. There was the waiter, and it certainly looked like Eyebrows. And there he was again at the ski hill. And there was Nish tossing his snowball.

"It's me he wants," Nish said, almost bragging.

"But why break into our rooms?" Travis asked.

"I don't know. Maybe he meant to play a trick on me but couldn't figure out which bed was mine."

"That hardly takes a rocket scientist to figure out," countered Sarah. "Just look for the unmade one with all the clothes dumped on the floor."

"Well, what then?" shot back Nish. "You tell us."

Sarah shook her head. "I don't know. There's something to this, though. Travis is right."

Several times they went over the tape. A waiter. Two men unloading a snowmobile and a sled. No poison. No explosives. Nothing.

"I still think we should show it to the police," said Travis.

"Show what?" Nish asked. "There's nothing there."

Travis sighed. He and his friends were missing something, he was certain, but he didn't know what.

"We better get going," said Sarah. "We've got a game at two."

This time the Screech Owls were up against the Matsumoto Sharks, a much better team than the Sapporo Mighty Ducks. Big Hat was almost filled for the match, and the sound when the Sharks came out onto the ice was almost as loud as if an NHL team had arrived. No one booed, however, when the Owls came out after them. The Owls' parents cheered from one corner, where they were all sitting together with their Screech Owls banners and Canadian flags, and the rest of the packed rink applauded, politely, as if the Owls had come to Nagano for a spelling bee instead of a hockey tournament.

The Sharks passed well and weren't afraid of shooting. There was no sense here of older *sempai* or younger *koohai* players. And the goalie, from what the Owls could gather during warm-up, was excellent, with a lightning-fast glove hand.

"I should be playing the point," Nish said to Travis during the warm-up. "We're going to need my shot."

Travis nodded. Nish might be right. But Muck still had him playing backup goal, so Travis didn't think there was any chance Nish would get into this game. If the Owls were going to win, they'd need Jenny in net all the way.

Muck started Andy's line, just to surprise the Sharks. Andy's line checked wonderfully, but they were slow compared to Sarah's line, and when Muck called for a change on the fly, it seemed to catch the Sharks off guard.

Dmitri leapt over the boards and took off for the far side of the rink, looping fast just as Sarah picked up a loose puck and rattled it hard off the boards so it flew ahead of Dmitri and beat him over the red line. No icing – and Dmitri was almost free.

Travis joined the rush. There was one defender back, and he didn't seem sure what to do: chase Dmitri or block the potential pass.

Dmitri solved his opponent's dilemma by cutting right across the ice, straight at the back-pedalling defenceman. The defender went for Dmitri, and Dmitri let him catch him, but he left the puck behind in a perfect drop pass.

Travis read the play perfectly, and picked up the sitting puck to burst in on goal. A head fake, a dipped shoulder, and the Sharks' goaltender went down.

Travis backhanded the puck high and hard – right off the crossbar!

The ring of metal was followed by a huge gasp throughout Big Hat. The goal light went on by mistake, but the players knew Travis hadn't scored.

The defenceman who'd been fooled picked up the puck and backhanded it high, nearly hitting the clock.

The puck slapped down past centre, and was scooped up by a Sharks forward in full flight. A clear breakaway!

Jenny came wiggling out to cut off the angle. The forward faked a slapshot, delayed while Jenny committed to blocking the shot, and then held on until he had swept farther around her, lofting an easy wristshot into the empty net.

Travis came off and looked down the bench toward Nish. His friend had his goalie glove over his face, afraid to look for fear Muck might be signalling him to go in.

"Defence stays back," Muck said calmly. "That doesn't happen again, understand?"

Everyone understood. There would be no more breakaways.

Little Simon Milliken got the Owls moving later in the period when he cut off a cross-blueline pass and broke up centre, a Sharks defenceman chasing frantically.

Simon waited until the last moment, and instead of shooting, dropped the puck back between the chasing defenceman's legs, perfectly on Liz's stick.

The play caught the Sharks' goaltender off guard. He'd counted on Simon going to his backhand and was now caught with the far side open.

Liz fired the puck hard and true, the net bulging as a huge cheer went up from the little Canadian section.

Heading into the third period, the score was tied 3–3 when Sarah took matters into her own hands. First, she set Travis up for an easy tap-in on a beautiful end-to-end rush. Then she sent Dmitri in on a breakaway, and he did his usual one fake and roofed a backhand. Then Sarah herself scored into the empty Sharks net in the final minute.

Owls 6, Sharks 3. But it had been a lot closer than it looked. They had won, yes, but no one felt good about how they had played. The Screech Owls had looked sloppy on defence, and defence was an area of the game in which they all took enormous pride.

"We play like that against Lake Placid," Muck said in the dressing room, "and we won't have a chance."

Muck and Mr. Dillinger had scouted the Lake Placid Olympians when they'd played the night before. A strong team with excellent skaters and one tremendous playmaker, the Olympians, Muck figured, would be as strong an opposition as the Owls had ever faced.

"We play like that again, and we won't have a chance," Muck repeated.

No one said a word. Travis knew that Muck was looking around the room. He could sense that Muck had looked at Jenny and wondered if the Owls would be in better shape if Jeremy were with them. He knew that Muck had looked, as well, at Nish and wondered if perhaps they shouldn't have Nish and his big shot playing out instead of sitting on the bench in goaltending gear he barely knew how to put on.

But Muck could hardly change things now. If he did anything with Nish, Jenny would think that Muck didn't have enough faith in her, which would only make her more nervous. He had to stick with Jenny, and was forced, also, to leave Nish where he was.

"If Lake Placid wins tonight, it's going to be them and us in the final," Muck said, finally. "Do you think you're ready for it?"

No one spoke. Travis knew, as captain, he had to say something.

"We can do it," he said.

"We'll win," said Sarah.

"Good," said Muck. "That's what I want to hear."

But did he believe it? Travis wondered.

More important, did the Owls believe it?

14

TRAVIS HAD NEVER KNOWN NISH TO TAKE HIS studies so seriously. Every morning, when the Screech Owls didn't have a game or a practice, Nish was off with Mr. Imoo, either at the Zenkoji Temple or at a special *dojo* near the Olympic Village where Mr. Imoo trained several students in the strange art of the Indonesian "force shield."

Nish seemed filled with wisdom, even if he couldn't yet curve spoons or, for that matter, even convince one of Sarah's hairpins to bend a bit when he tickled it one day at lunch. Other students, Nish claimed, could break bricks and boards with their foreheads.

"There's a master in Indonesia," he said, "who can pick a bullet out of the air."

"A *shot* bullet?" Fahd asked.

Nish looked at Fahd as if he were an idiot. Everyone else looked at Nish as if he were making it up.

But Travis had to give his old friend credit. Nish was applying himself to this newfound interest much more than Nish had ever worked on math or science or English. Mr. Imoo seemed to understand Nish perfectly. He was even starting to make jokes about Nish stinking up the *dojo*.

Nish didn't mind. He was going to master this. Before the trip was out, he was determined to find his own force shield.

The Screech Owls had one more practice at Big Hat before the championship weekend. Muck ran some drills and had the Owls practise tip-ins on Jenny at one end and on Nish at the other. He had his reasons.

"Lake Placid made the final easily," Muck told them later in the dressing room. "They are an excellent team. They know how to get traffic in front of the net, and they know how to get point shots on the net for tip-ins and rebounds. That's why we were working on the same thing ourselves today. I want to get our goalies comfortable with what they'll be facing."

Muck finished talking, but he didn't look finished. He walked around the room and cleared his throat a couple of times. No one said a word. Even Nish sat quietly, his goalie mask still on top of his head.

"Mr. Dillinger will talk to you now," he said.

Muck walked toward the dressing room and held the door open for Mr. Dillinger to come in. Mr. Dillinger looked worried. He was rubbing his hands together.

"I've just met with the Nagano police," said Mr. Dillinger.

"Any word on the break-ins?" Fahd asked.

"No," Mr. Dillinger said, shaking his head.

"More blowfish?" Fahd asked.

Mr. Dillinger shook his head again.

"The avalanche," he said. "They've found some evidence that it was set off deliberately. They found dynamite blasting caps up the hill."

Travis snapped back, striking his head lightly on the wall behind him. *Dynamite!* So that was why the avalanche had started with such a bang. It was an explosion!

"What for?" Andy asked with a slight tremor in his voice. "Were they trying to kill us?"

"The police don't know," said Mr. Dillinger. "But they want us to be very careful from here on out. They don't know if there's any connection between the break-ins and the avalanche – maybe even the murder of the mayor – but they're afraid to take anything for granted. From now on, we stay together in groups of at least three, all right? And we stick to the Village and the hockey rink."

He looked around the room, his big eyes pleading for understanding. Mr. Dillinger looked very hurt. This was hardly the way the trip to Japan had been planned to go.

Travis had never heard the phone ring in his room before. It caught him by surprise. He'd been brushing his teeth, and Nish had been sitting, cross-legged, on his bed, his eyes closed, deep in concentration.

It took a moment for Travis to locate it. There was a desk against one wall and the telephone was on the floor beside it, covered by several sweaty T-shirts belonging to Nish.

He picked it up. But what should he say? "Hello"? Or "*Moshi moshi*"?

"Hel-lo," he said, uncertain.

"Travis – that you?"

"Yeah . . . *Data?*"

"It's me. Nish there?"

Travis looked over at his roommate, still seemingly deep in a trance.

"I think so."

"Good. Get down here. *Quick!*"

Travis had no idea what had Data so worked up, but it was clear from his voice that he was very, very excited about something.

"C'mon," Travis said to Nish. "That was Data. He needs us."

Nish made no sign of moving.

"*Hey!*" Travis yelled. Nish's eyes popped open. He was back in the real world.

"What's up?"

"Data needs us – let's go!"

To get to Data's ground-floor apartment, they had to cut across the courtyard and through the tent where the teams ate their meals. They picked up Sarah and Jenny along the way.

"We're supposed to be in groups of three or more," Travis explained. "Data needs us."

The four Screech Owls found Data's door unlocked when they got there. They let themselves in.

Data was in his wheelchair. He had a small television on top of the desk and a tiny video cassette recorder beside it.

"The man at the desk sent this to me with some movies to watch," Data explained. "But I set it up to see what our tape looked like so far."

He had the tape paused at the point where Nish threw the snowball at Eyebrows.

"Did you check for explosives?" Nish asked. "I bet it was Eyebrows who started the avalanche."

"It might have been," said Data. "But there's nothing there. See for yourself."

Data ran the footage of the men pulling up in the Toyota 4×4 and unloading the snowmobile and sled. The Owls pulled up chairs or sat on the edge of Data's bed and went over it carefully several times, but there was nothing remarkable. Whatever was in the sled was out of sight. It could have been dynamite; it could just as easily have been blankets or shovels. No way would the video ever convince the police that Eyebrows had started the avalanche.

"There's nothing there, see?"

"We see," said Sarah. "But you found something, didn't you, Data?"

Data looked at her and nodded.

He seemed a little frightened.

"I want you to watch this."

Data rewound the tape, then stopped it and pressed "play" to see where he was. It was the banquet, near the end.

"Here's where Eyebrows runs me over!" announced Nish.

"It's before that," said Data, pushing the "rewind" button again.

When he had found the right spot, Data turned to the four friends. "I'll just play it straight," he said. "You tell me if you see anything."

The four leaned closer to the television and Data pushed "play."

The picture cleared. It was the beginning of the banquet. They saw the teams heading for their places. There were shots of the Screech Owls sitting down.

The camera then scanned the head table, just as Muck and the others were taking their places.

Sho Fujiwara, the man in charge of Japanese hockey, was reaching out an arm toward Muck. He was pulling him over, smiling and gesturing for Muck to sit.

Data hit "pause."

"See anything?" he asked.

"Muck and Sho," said Jenny. "They sat together, remember?"

"What about it?" asked Nish. "I saw nothing."

"I'm going to run it again," said Data.

The machine whirred back, clicked, then started again at just the right place.

Sho Fujiwara was standing at the table. He saw Muck and called him over. They seemed like old pals, happy to be together. It made sense for them to sit side by side.

As Muck stepped up onto the raised platform and headed toward his new friend, Sho deftly switched a couple of the place cards showing who should sit where.

Data stopped the machine.

"See?" he asked.

"He changed the seating plan so Muck could sit beside him," Travis said. "Big deal."

"Your point?" asked Sarah.

"Watch again," said Data. "You can read the place cards if you look closely."

He played the same sequence again. Sho called Muck over. Sho switched the seating around.

Data stopped the machine.

"The mayor was not sitting where he was supposed to."

Again he played the sequence.

Data was right! To get Muck beside him, Sho had to switch the names around on the head table. Muck had ended up beside him, but the mayor had bumped Mr. Ikura over one place.

"The blowfish wasn't meant for the mayor," said Data. "Whoever the murderer is, he wanted to kill Mr. Ikura."

They stared at the machine on "pause," nothing moving on the screen, but images racing in their minds.

Data was right. If it hadn't been for the switching of places, the mayor would have been one seat over.

Someone must have brought the blowfish out to a designated spot at the head table, the place where Mr. Ikura was supposed to be sitting.

The waiter? Is that why he ran — because he'd realized the mistake too late?

And is that why Eyebrows was up to no good at Mr. Ikura's ski hill?

"We better take this to Mr. Dillinger," said Sarah. "He'll want the police to see this."

15

THE POLICE ARRIVED WITHIN FIVE MINUTES OF Mr. Dillinger's call. They brought translators, and they even had a precision video player that could freeze a single frame of tape so that it looked like a sharp, crystal-clear photograph. Travis couldn't believe how efficient they were.

Nish was in his glory, bowing left and right to every Japanese person who looked like he or she might be even remotely connected to the investigation. He acted as if he alone had solved the crime – even if, so far, no crime at all had been solved.

The police interviewed Muck about the switch in places at the head table. They brought in Sho Fujiwara and interviewed him separately, and then Sho and Muck together. They interviewed Data alone, Travis alone, Nish alone, Sarah alone, and then talked to them in a group. Nish was taken to a special investigative van that had pulled up outside the Olympic Village and was asked to look at possible suspects on a computer screen. He claimed he had found Eyebrows within a matter of minutes.

The police packed up and left. They made no mention of what they were going to do. No hint of what might happen now. Nothing.

Six hours later, they were back — with the full story.

The man the Owls called Eyebrows — "I identified him," bragged Nish — was a well-known *yakuza*, a Japanese gangster. "*Yakuza* means good for nothing," explained Sho Fujiwara, who was also called back for the meeting with the police. "We have bad people here in Japan, too."

Eyebrows had been hired to do the murder. But the mayor of Nagano was never intended to be the victim. The man they wanted to kill was Mr. Ikura, the owner of the ski hill. The blowfish plot had, apparently, been Eyebrows' idea, and he had botched it so badly — dressing up like a waiter and serving the poisonous dish to the wrong person at the head table — that he'd been scrambling to make up for it ever since.

The avalanche was also Eyebrows' idea. He was worried that the very thugs who had hired him might now want to kill him for botching the job, so he'd tried to frighten Mr. Ikura into selling off.

That turned out to be a huge mistake, and a key break in the case for the police. Mr. Ikura had been under enormous pressure to sell to a corporation, but had refused to do so. This company had plans to turn the site of the Olympic skiing and snowboarding competitions into a major international tourist complex for the very rich, complete with a huge chalet development, that would have closed off the hill to the likes of the Owls and the people of Nagano. Mr. Ikura could have made millions by selling, but chose not to.

He was saying no to the wrong people, apparently. When they couldn't convince him to sell, they hired Eyebrows to kill him, believing that Mr. Ikura's heirs would quickly agree to the sale.

If the death looked accidental, no one would ever connect it with the sale. Eyebrows' idea was that the blowfish poisoning would look like a heart attack. But when he accidentally killed the mayor of Nagano, he aroused the police's suspicions. The sudden death of a well-known politician could not go uninvestigated, and the police had ordered an autopsy that discovered the blowfish.

Even so, there was still nothing to throw suspicion on the big corporation and its plans for Mr. Ikura's ski lodge. It wasn't until the avalanche that the pieces of the puzzle finally started to fall into place. First, the avalanche was out of season, and while looking for the cause they had found the dynamite caps not far from where they figured the slide had started.

The final, essential, clue was Data's video. It not only placed Eyebrows at both the banquet and the ski hill — with no real proof of wrong-doing, the police pointed out — it also showed the switch of places at the head table.

Once the police knew that the intended victim had been Mr. Ikura, and that the avalanche had been deliberate, they quickly came up with a pretty good idea of what had happened.

Data's tape had also helped the police track down Eyebrows' accomplice. The man helping Eyebrows unload the snowmobile and sled from the Toyota 4 × 4 had cracked almost immediately. He hadn't even known what Eyebrows had in the sled. And once he realized he was caught up in a murder, he told them everything he knew — including where to find Eyebrows.

"He's in jail right now," Sho told the Owls. "And he'll probably spend the rest of his life there.

"The City of Nagano — all Japan, for that matter — is deeply indebted to you, Mr. Data. We thank you and your friends."

Data was a hero. The newspapers came to do stories on him. Television stations came to interview him.

"I identified the guy," Nish told each and every one of the reporters as they and their film crews arrived at the Olympic Village.

But no one was interested in Nish. The hockey player in the wheelchair — the master sleuth, the Canadian Sherlock Holmes – was the biggest story in Japan. Next to Anne of Green Gables, he was, for a few days, the most-beloved young Canadian in all of Japan.

"I identified the guy," Nish kept saying.

16

SARAH WAS FIRST IN THE BIG HAT DRESSING room. When Travis made his way in, he could tell at once that she was pumped for the championship game against the Lake Placid Olympians. Her eyes seemed on fire.

"One for each of you," she said as she handed each arriving player a small plastic package.

"Hide them until I give the signal."

Nish, as always, was last into the room, dragging and pushing and half kicking his hockey bag. He dropped his sticks against the wall, letting them fall against the others that had been set there so carefully and sending them crashing to the floor like falling dominoes.

No one said a word. Nish looked around at them, seemingly disappointed that no one had noticed him.

He had an open can of Sweat and took a huge slug of it before he sat down, burping loudly as the gas backed up in his throat.

Even with your eyes shut, Travis thought to himself, you would know when Nish had arrived in a hockey dressing room. The crashing sticks.

The dragging bag on the floor. The burping. The long, lazy zip of the hockey bag, and the terrible sweaty odour that rose up from inside. The rest of the Owls had given up asking him to wash his equipment. "Sweat is my good-luck charm," he said. "Smell bad, play good."

Nish took off his jacket and shirt, stood up, burped again, and walked to the end of the dressing room, where he slammed the washroom door: part of his hockey ritual, as certain as fresh tape on his stick, as sure as the drop of the puck.

"*Now!*" Sarah hissed.

Everyone dipped into the little packages she had handed out. Some began giggling when they saw what it was that Sarah had brought for them. They had to move quickly.

The toilet flushed, and from behind the closed door Nish groaned with the exaggerated satisfaction he always displayed at this moment.

The door banged open, Nish pumping a fist in the air – and then he saw the Owls.

Sarah had issued each team member a face mask, the kind the Japanese wore to keep out pollution. They were all wearing them, all sitting in their stalls, staring at Nish over the white gauze that covered their noses and mouths.

"What's *that* supposed to mean?" Nish said.

"Think about it," Sarah said, her voice muffled.

Muck came in pushing Data. Data started giggling when he saw the masks, but Muck said nothing. Nothing ever seemed to surprise Muck, thought Travis. Not even Nish.

Mr. Dillinger came in and did a double take at the kids in their masks, but he, too, said nothing. He went about his business, filling the water bottles, getting the tape ready, making sure there were pucks for the warm-up.

Sarah removed her mask and the others followed. Muck waited until everyone was ready, their minds back on the game.

"The rink is full," said Muck. "The whole town came out to cheer Data – that's what I think – but they deserve to see some good North American hockey, too. If hockey's going to take off in this country, they're going to have to see what a great game it can be.

"I want a clean game. I want a good game. I want these people to know how much we appreciate them coming out to watch."

The door opened again and Mr. Imoo popped his head in. He was grinning ear to ear, the gap in his teeth almost exactly the width of a puck.

"Good show today, Owls," he said.

Mr. Imoo turned to his prize pupil, Nish, who was beaming.

"Nish," he said. "I think you're ready."

Travis looked at Muck, who cocked an eyebrow. What did Muck think? Travis wondered.

That Mr. Imoo thought Nish was "ready" to play goal? Not likely, not against the Lake Placid Olympians, that was for sure.

Travis glanced over at Nish, who seemed to have assumed a new, calm look. It was no longer the Nish who was always desperate to be the centre of attention. It was a Nish filled with poise and confidence.

Travis couldn't help it: he wished Nish wasn't playing goal. They would need him on defence, and even if Muck never put him in, Nish wouldn't be much use to the Owls sitting at the end of the bench.

But he also knew there was no choice. Tournament rules were rules: they had to have a second goalie. If only Jeremy had been able to come. He hoped Jenny was going to have a good game.

"Okay?" Muck said. He was staring at Travis.

Travis understood the signal. As captain, he was to lead them out onto the ice.

"*Let's go!*" Travis shouted, standing up and yanking on his helmet.

"*Screech Owls!*" Sarah called as she stood.

"*Let's do it!*" called Lars.

"*Owls!*"

"*Owls!*"

"*Owls!*"

17

TRAVIS HAD NEVER BEEN IN SUCH A GAME!

He had played in front of large crowds before – larger even than this one, which filled Big Hat – but never in front of a crowd that cheered every single thing that happened.

The biggest cheer, so far, had been when the crowd had first noticed Data coming out onto the ice, pushed by Mr. Dillinger. They had risen to their feet in a long standing ovation. Data had waved and smiled and probably wished it would be over with, but Travis knew how much this meant to his friend. The Japanese were all grateful for what he had done.

He had heard crowds cheer and boo before, but never one that seemed to find no fault with anything. They played no favourites. They did not boo the referee or the linesmen. They cheered the goals and the saves equally. They were cheering, he supposed, for *hockey*.

And the hockey was fantastic. The Screech Owls and the Lake Placid Olympians were evenly matched. Jenny was outstanding in the Owls' goal, but so, too, was the little guy playing net for the Olympians. He had an unbelievable glove hand, and had twice robbed Dmitri on clean breakaways, the Screech Owls forward going both times to his special backhand move that almost always meant the goaltender's water bottle flying off the top of the net and a Screech Owls goal.

Muck was matching lines with the Lake Placid coach, and he seemed to be enjoying the game as much as anyone. Mr. Dillinger was handling the defence door and Data the forwards', so every time Travis came off or went on, he felt Data pat him as he passed.

Sarah's line was on against the top Olympians' line – Sarah the playmaker matched with Lake Placid's top playmaker, a big, lanky kid with such a long reach no one seemed capable of checking him. The big playmaker had two good wingers, too, which meant that Travis had to pay far more attention to defence than offence.

Muck wanted them to shut down the big Lake Placid line. It made sense. Sarah was the best checker on the team, by far, when she put her mind to it – and when Sarah was sent out in a checking role, she seemed to take as much pride in stopping goals as she did in making them happen.

The Owls scored first when Andy's line got a lucky bounce at the blueline. The puck hit some bad ice as it was sent back for a point shot and bounced over the defenceman's stick and out to centre. Andy, with his long stride, got the jump on both defence and broke in alone. The Lake Placid goaltender made a wonderful stop on Andy, stacking his pads as Andy tried to pull him out and dump it into the far side, but the rebound went straight to little Simon Milliken, who found he had an empty net staring at him.

Two minutes later, the game was tied up. The big Lake Placid playmaker went end to end, losing Sarah on a twisting play at his own blue-line and faking Wilson brilliantly as he broke in. The big Olympian dumped the puck in a saucer pass to one side of Wilson and curled around him on the other side, picking up his own pass to come in alone on Jenny. Two big fakes, and Jenny was sprawled out of the position and the puck was in the back of the net.

Between the first and second period, Muck told Sarah to step it up. "You're taking your checking too seriously," he told her. "If you have the puck, he can't have it."

Sarah knew what Muck meant. Her line started the second period, and she snicked the puck out of the air as it fell, sending it back to Wilson.

Dmitri broke hard for the far blueline, cutting toward centre.

Wilson hit him perfectly. Dmitri took the pass and sent it back between his own legs to Travis, who stepped into it as he crossed the blueline.

Sarah was slapping the ice with her stick. Travis didn't even look. He flipped the puck into empty space, knowing she would be there in an instant – and she was.

Sarah was in free. The goaltender began backing up, preparing for a fake, but she shot almost at once, completely fooling the goalie and finding the net just over his left shoulder.

"That's more like it," Muck said when Sarah and Travis got back to the bench. He put a big hand on each player's neck as they gathered their breath. Travis liked nothing better in the world than to feel Muck do that. The coach didn't even think about it, probably, but it meant everything.

Andy then scored on a pretty play, sent in by Simon on a neat pass when Simon was falling with the puck. Andy went to his backhand and slipped the shot low through the sharp little goalie's pads.

Into the third period, the Olympians began to press.

The big playmaker came straight up centre and swept around Sarah, who dived after him, her stick accidentally sweeping away his skates.

The referee's whistle blew.

Travis cringed. The Owls could hardly afford to lose their best player just now. But Sarah was going off. The referee signalled "tripping" to the timekeeper, the penalty door box swung open, and Sarah, slamming her stick once in anger at herself, headed for it.

The crowd cheered politely. Travis giggled. He couldn't help himself.

The Olympians needed only one shot to score on the power play. It came in from the point, and Jenny had it all the way, but just at the last moment the big Lake Placid playmaker reached his stick blade out just enough to tick the puck, and it changed direction and flipped over her outstretched pad.

Screech Owls 3, Olympians 2.

The Lake Placid team started to press even harder. Travis wondered if they could hold them back. *If only they had Nish on the ice. If only Nish wasn't sitting there, on the end of the bench, in his goalie gear . . .*

The Olympians' strategy was to crash the net, hoping to set up shots from the point like the one that had gone in on the power play. When the defence shot, the forwards tried to screen Jenny in front, attempting either to tip another shot or allow one to slip through without Jenny seeing it coming.

The game was getting rough, but the referee was calling nothing.

The right defenceman had the puck, and Travis dived to block the shot, shutting his eyes instinctively as he hit the ice.

He waited for the puck to crash into him — but nothing happened. When he opened his eyes, he saw the defenceman deftly step around him, closing in even tighter for the shot.

The defenceman took a mighty slapshot. Jenny's glove hand snaked out. *She had it!*

But then the big playmaker crashed into her.

They hit, and Jenny gave, flying toward the corner, the big playmaker going with her and crashing hard on top of her into the boards.

The whistle blew.

Mr. Dillinger was already over the boards, racing and slipping on the ice, a towel in one hand.

Jenny was groaning. She was moving her legs but still flat on her back, the air knocked out of her.

"*No penalty?*" Jenny was asking the referee.

The referee was shaking his head. "Your own man hit him into her," the referee said.

The referee was pointing at Wilson. Wilson didn't argue. It was true. He had been trying to clear the big playmaker out from in front of the net, and he had put his shoulder into him just when Jenny made her spectacular save.

Travis glided in closer to Jenny. He was exhausted, his breath coming in huge gulps. He knew that this time, this game, he was covered in sweat.

Mr. Dillinger was leaning over Jenny.

He looked up, catching the referee's eye.

"Just the wind knocked out," he said. "But she's hurt her arm, too."

"You'll have to replace her," said the referee. "We have to get this game in."

Mr. Dillinger winced.

Travis winced.

If Jenny couldn't play, that meant only one thing.

Nish was going in!

Jenny was up and holding her arm cautiously. She had tears rolling down her cheeks, but whether that was from the pain or the fact that she couldn't go on, Travis couldn't say.

The big playmaker brushed by him, reaching out to tap Jenny's pads.

"Sorry about that," he said. "You played great."

Jenny smiled through her tears. Travis could tell how much that meant to her, the best player she'd ever faced showing her that kind of respect. Travis was impressed. It was a very classy thing for the big Olympian to do.

"I'm ready," Nish announced.

Muck didn't seem convinced. But he had no choice. He stared long and hard at his new goal-tender, who was standing in front of the bench, his mask on top of his head, spraying water directly into his face.

"Do what you can," Muck said. "And don't worry about it."

But Nish was into it. He sprayed the water, spat another mouthful out, yanked down his mask as if he were a fighter pilot about to take off, jumped over the red line, jumped over the blueline, skated to where Mr. Imoo was standing, clapping, smashed his stick into the glass, then turned and headed for his net.

A quick few words with his goal posts, and he was ready to go.

Nish, the *samurai* goaltender.

It was over, Travis figured. They could barely hold the Lake Placid team with Jenny playing her best. How could they hold them off now with Nish in net? Nish, who didn't know the first thing about playing goal.

"Let's just get it over with fast," Sarah said. "And hope we don't embarrass ourselves too badly."

The Lake Placid team seemed to take new energy from the fact that Nish was in net. Whether it was because they were impressed by his hot-dog moves or because they knew how weak he was, Travis couldn't tell. But suddenly the Olympians were even stronger.

Sarah, however, had her own ideas. If Lake Placid was going to score, the big playmaker wouldn't be the one to do it. She began playing as furiously as her opponent, sticking to him with every move, lifting his stick when he reached for passes, and stepping in his way whenever he tried for the fast break.

It didn't seem to matter. The Olympians tied the game on their very first shot, a long bouncing puck from centre ice that skipped funny and went in through Nish's skates.

"Oh, no!" Sarah said as they sat on the bench watching.

"This is going to get ugly," said Travis.

Next shift, one of the quicker Lake Placid forwards broke up-ice, and the big playmaker put a perfect breakaway pass on his stick.

But Nish took the forward by surprise, coming out to block the shot like a defenceman instead of waiting on it like a goalie, and the shot bounced away harmlessly.

"*Way to go, Nish!*" Travis found himself yelling as he turned back up-ice.

Nish seemed to find himself over the next few minutes. It wasn't pretty – it wasn't like anything anyone had ever seen before – but it worked. He kicked, he turned backwards, he threw himself, head-first, at shots.

And not one got past him.

"That idiot's playing his heart out!" Sarah said when her line came off for a rest.

"I know," said Travis.

"We owe him a goal for all this, you know."

"I know."

Next shift, Sarah raced back to pick the puck away from Nish's crease. He was flat on his back, looking like he was making snow angels instead of playing goal, and he cheered her as she took the puck out of harm's way and up-ice.

"*Do it, Sarah!*"

Sarah played a quick give-and-go with Dmitri, who fed the puck back to her just as she hit the Lake Placid blueline. She slipped past the defenceman and curled so sharply in the corner, the other defenceman lost his footing and crashed into the backboards.

Travis had his stick down before he even imagined what he might do. It was as if his stick was thinking for itself. It was down flat and out in front of him, and Sarah's hard pass hit it perfectly, a laser beam from the corner.

Travis didn't even have to shoot – the puck cracked against his stick and snapped off it, directly into the open side of the Lake Placid net.

Travis had been mobbed before, but never like this.

He felt them piling on, one by one, and then the huge weight of the goaltender, who had skated the length of the ice to join the pile: the *samurai* goaltender.

"*We did it! We did it! We did it!*" Nish was screaming.

"We've done nothing yet," corrected Sarah. "There's still five minutes to go."

"Don't worry about it," Nish said. "I've got everything under control."

It seemed he had. The game started up again with the Owls leading 4–3, and Nish took everything the Olympians could fire at him.

With a minute and a half to go, and a face-off in the Owls' end, Lake Placid pulled their goaltender.

"Sarah's line," Muck said. "And nothing foolish. We protect the lead, okay?"

They understood. No trying for the grandstand empty-net goal. If it came, it came, but their first job was to protect Nish and the lead.

Sarah dumped the puck out, but not far enough for icing. Travis and Dmitri went on the forecheck, twice causing the defence to turn back.

They were killing the clock. So long as the Olympians couldn't rush, the Owls didn't care how long they held on to the puck.

The big playmaker circled back, picking up a puck the Lake Placid defence dropped for him.

He was in full flight.

Travis had the first chance and foolishly went for the poke check. One quick move of the big playmaker's stick and he was past Travis and moving away from Dmitri.

Sarah stuck with him, leading him off along the boards and into the corner, where he stopped with the puck.

Ten seconds to go!

Sarah moved toward him and he backhanded the puck off the boards, stepping around her and picking the puck off on the rebound. A play worthy of Sarah herself.

He circled the net, Nish wrongly stabbing for the puck as he passed by the far side.

Nish's goal stick flew away to the corner!

The big playmaker fired the puck to the point and crashed the net.

The shot came in. Nish kicked it away.

Wilson and Sarah hit the big playmaker at exactly the same time, sending him crashing into Nish, who fell hard.

Nish's glove shot to the other corner!

Three seconds to go!

He had no stick. He had no glove.

And the defenceman was winding up for a second shot!

Travis had never seen Nish move so fast. In a flash he was back on his skates, crouching to face the shot.

The defenceman slammed into the puck, sending it soaring off his stick toward the net. Sarah dived, the puck clipping off her back and heading now for the top corner.

A bare hand snaked out, and the puck seemed to stop in mid-air!

The horn blew!

The Screech Owls had won the Junior Olympics!

After that, Travis could remember only bits of what happened.

The Screech Owls – Muck and Mr. Dillinger and Data included – had hit the ice instantly, racing to congratulate Nish, who simply sat back in his crease, holding the puck above his head as if it were some great trick he'd pulled out of his own ear.

They mobbed him.

The doors at the far end of Big Hat had opened up and an official delegation, led by Sho Fujiwara, came out. They were followed by a long line of women dressed in beautiful traditional costumes, each carrying a cushion, and each cushion holding a medal.

They had played the Canadian anthem, with the Canadian flag going up on a huge banner.

Everyone in the building had cheered.

After the anthem, the Lake Placid Olympians formed a line and shook hands with the Screech Owls.

Jenny went through the line with her right hand in a sling. When she came to the big play-maker, he dropped his sticks and gloves and hugged her.

There were cameras on the ice now, and they captured it all.

Nish was at the Zamboni entrance. He was hauling Mr. Imoo out onto the ice. Mr. Imoo, his missing teeth more noticeable than ever, was sliding and hurrying out to join in the celebration with his star pupil.

Nish took the puck he'd saved – "The Greatest Save in the History of International Hockey," he would later call it – and gave it to Mr. Imoo, who seemed honoured.

"I caught it with the force shield," he explained.

Travis, the Screech Owls captain, was now face-to-face with the big playmaker, the Lake Placid Olympians captain.

Travis looked up. The big playmaker was grinning. He looked as if he'd won himself.

"Great game," he said.

"Maybe the best ever," Travis said.

They shook hands.

"Ever see a crowd like this?" the big playmaker asked.

"Never."

"We should do something for them," the big playmaker said.

It took them only a moment to decide what.

They waited until the medals had been given out. Travis felt the gold around his neck and watched while the silver medals were awarded to the Lake Placid team.

Then, on a signal from the big Olympian, Travis motioned for all the Owls to skate to centre ice with him.

He went and got Muck, who came reluctantly. Mr. Dillinger pushed Data.

The big playmaker gathered all his team and coaches as well.

Then at centre ice they turned, first to one side of the rink, then the other, then the far ends, while the fans continued to stand and applaud.

And they bowed.

Arigato.

A thank-you to Japan.

THE SCREECH OWLS SERIES

DATE DUE
DATE DE RETOUR

MAR 2 0 2008	
MAR 2 0 2008	
NOV 1 6 2009	